Cimarron Secrets

By

Lori Herter

Table of Contents

Cover art by SelfPubBookCovers.com/Shardel

CIMARRON SECRETS

By

Lori Herter

Chapter One

Annie Carmichael made a rash decision in the hour before dawn of what was to be her wedding day. Now a runaway bride, she couldn't believe the sheer joy she felt as she rode across the moonlit Arizona desert with Rafael de la Vega on his magnificent leopard Appaloosa.

As the mid-October night wind cooled her face and blew through her long brown hair, Annie understood how a prisoner must feel escaping from jail. Her wedding to Brent Logan would not take place at four p.m. at his big ranch house that afternoon. She wondered what Brent would do. Cancel the catered dinner, or invite guests to stay and eat? And gossip, no doubt.

Well, that was really none of her business anymore. Annie had a new life to look forward to, with Rafael. Yet she knew it would be a challenge to live with her true love, her soul mate.

The handsome, black-haired, charismatic man she'd chosen, Rafael, was a vampire.

"Easy, Esperanza," Rafael said, as he pulled back on the reins. The white Appaloosa, dappled with black spots, slowed as they approached Rafael's ranch house, located several miles from the Logan spread.

Brent Logan and Rafael de la Vega owned bordering properties, but they had never met. Brent once told Annie that old-timers called Rafael a *cimarron*, a timeworn cowboy term for a loner who has little to do with others. She'd looked up the word and discovered that in Spanish, cimarron meant *wild* or *untamed*. Both descriptions fit, she'd learned over the last couple of months. Her secret nighttime trysts with Rafael had been thrillingly untamed.

"We must hurry," he said. "I can feel dawn approaching."

Rafael dismounted his horse with the ease of a gymnast. Raising his muscular arms, he carefully helped Annie to the ground. He began leading Esperanza to a corral next to the Spanish-tiled stucco house.

"Go on inside," he told Annie. "I left the front door unlocked."

She walked to the big oak door and entered the blue-and-white-tiled entry hall. The house stood cold and silent. Lights from the rustic wood chandelier overhead lit the room in a shadowy way. Still dressed in her long, pale blue nightgown, she began to feel more chilled than she had while riding across the desert.

She'd been trying to sleep in her room at the Logan ranch when she'd heard hoof beats outside, and then Rafael had appeared at her window. He'd begged her not to marry Brent. Rafael implored her to come away with him instead. The crux of Annie's dilemma had made her hesitate. Did she want a conventional life as a cattle rancher's wife? Or did she want to be with Rafael, who had been a Spanish conquistador? In 1540, on his thirtieth birthday, a gypsy curse had caused him to die and rise as a vampire. An immortal who had not seen the sun in nearly five hundred years, Rafael had loved her in ways no mortal man ever could.

Inez Garcia, Brent's longtime cook, had heard noises in Annie's room, next to hers. When she came in to check and saw Rafael, she'd said, "You've come to claim Annie." Inez had known Rafael's dark secret for decades. Torn by her dilemma, Annie had asked Inez, what should she do? Annie had always wanted a family of her own. Yet she loved Rafael to distraction.

Inez had replied, "Can you be a good wife to Brent knowing Rafael exists, loving and needing you?"

Inez's pithy question had brought everything into focus. Instantly, Annie had realized she must be with Rafael no matter what, and so she'd run off with him.

And now here she was, at Rafael's home, dressed only in her thin nightgown, having left everything behind, anxiously waiting for Rafael to come inside before the sun rose. A rather stark beginning to her happily-ever-after.

The door opened and Rafael strode in, his boots softly clicking on the tile floor. Tall and muscular in his open-collared white shirt, his denim jeans covering his slim waist and hips, he moved in a languid way that belied his deft quickness and superhuman strength.

He took her by the hand. "I'll show you where I rest during the day. It's a hidden room. You will be the only one who knows, besides myself."

Annie understood how much he was trusting her to keep his grim secret. She cherished the fact that he put so much faith in her, and yet she began to feel nervous with a weighty new responsibility that seemed to be settling on her shoulders.

Rafael led her through the living room, through the dusty dining room with its large, bare table, into the kitchen. At the other end of the kitchen, past a modern, stainless steel refrigerator and an antiquated, avocado-hued stove and flat-bottomed sink, lay an old-fashioned walk-in pantry. As he led her in, Annie glanced about at the musty pine shelves along the walls, almost all of them empty. She saw only a small box of tea bags and a can of coffee, both gray with dust.

Rafael stopped at the far end of the narrow pantry and pulled something out of his pocket.

Annie saw it was an old-style metal key, long, with a jagged end to work the lock, and a decorative oval on the other end. "Where's the door?" she asked.

He pointed to a small keyhole almost unnoticeable beneath a shelf. The metal around the keyhole had been painted white to match the walls. He fit the key into the lock, turned it and pulled. A door so unobtrusive as to be practically invisible opened. With three small shelves attached to the door, when closed it simply looked like the narrow back wall of the pantry.

"Be careful," he told her. "There are ten steep steps." Rafael bent to pick up a flashlight sitting on the top step and switched on the beam of light. He stepped down, reaching back to take her arm to steady her. She carefully followed him down the stairs, picking up the hem of her nightgown to watch her feet as he shone light on each new step. There was no railing.

When they reached the bottom, he pointed his flashlight at a large object in the middle of what appeared to be a small, claustrophobic room with unpainted cement walls. The object on the cold cement floor was made of varnished pine. A rectangular box.

Annie drew in a sharp breath as she realized what it was.

He turned and looked her in the eye. "I told you I rest in my coffin during the day."

"I know, but . . . the reality of it . . ." Annie didn't finish. She nodded her head in a deliberate manner, accepting the plain truth of how Rafael had survived for centuries, knowing she had to be strong. "Y-you had this room specially built?"

"Many years ago. I made the coffin myself."

Annie nodded again, taking in a long breath. "It seems so bleak."

Rafael picked up a box of matches next to a tall, thick candle on the floor. "I suppose I should have put Spanish tiles on the walls." He struck the match and lit the candle. "Or at least painted them, but I never bothered. You can see now why I often like to rest in the kiva at the ruin. Rather more picturesque."

"Yes, it is," she agreed, trying to smile.

The kiva he spoke of was part of the Anasazi ruin located at the edge of Brent Logan's property that Annie, an Associate Professor of Archeology, was excavating. She'd first encountered Rafael there. Unknown to her at the time, he had the ability to shapeshift, and he'd appeared at dusk on two occasions as a wolf. Then, late one afternoon when she'd stayed past sundown, he'd met her in human form. He'd introduced himself and while he seemed a bit mysterious and unpredictable, she'd thought him to be a mortal male like any other man she'd ever met. But a few days later, she'd opened up the underground kiva when the sun was still overhead and discovered him there, lethargic and barely able to move or speak.

"It's time," Rafael said, handing her the flashlight. "I can sense the sun's rays growing stronger, even through these thick walls." He lifted the lid of the coffin, then turned to Annie, a moist glint in his eyes. "Will you still be here tonight? Or will you go back and marry Logan as planned? Have the normal life you wanted, instead of becoming the living partner of a vampire." He gave her a wistful smile. "A vampire who loves and treasures you above all else."

Tears welled in Annie's eyes. "I love you too much to leave you."

They embraced, but Annie could feel his powerful arms about her growing weak. He let her go and stepped into the coffin, stretching out on a thick Navaho blanket inside. She noticed the folded blanket was set over a layer of desert earth.

"You leave the candle burning while you sleep?" she asked.

"My substitute for the sun," he said, his voice fading. "Make yourself at home. Redecorate whatever you don't like. My darling Annie . . ." With the last of his strength, he paused and gave her an adoring look, then closed the lid over him.

Annie stood still for a long moment, stiff and shivering, feeling abandoned. The hidden room was even colder than the rest of the house. She climbed the stairs, left the flashlight on the top step and entered the pantry. Closing the door behind her, she wondered if Rafael had forgotten to lock himself in because she was there.

For months she'd furtively driven to his ranch house at two a.m. several nights a week for a few hours of overwhelming, blissfully addicting sex in his arms. But she knew little of his habits, how he existed, how he ran Rancho de la Noche, well-known to the equestrian world for the prize Appaloosa horses bred here.

Annie stepped into the kitchen, noticing its earth-toned, green-and-beige-tiled floor. Early morning light coming from the café-curtained window above the sink brightened the room, with its white cabinets and walls painted a pastel shade of green. She noticed the avocado-colored stove again and guessed it could date back to the 1960's. The large, flat-bottomed sink looked like it belonged in an old farmhouse. There was no dishwasher. Yet, surprisingly, the stainless steel refrigerator appeared to be new, or at least no more than a decade old.

Beginning to feel hungry for some breakfast, Annie opened it up. What she saw made her gasp and step backward, her hand covering her mouth. *Blood bags*. "Oh, my God . . ."

There were three of them neatly set side by side on the middle shelf of the otherwise spotlessly barren refrigerator. They were professionally labeled *Whole Blood* and had collection and expiration dates. The deep red liquid they held could easily be seen through the clear bags and up into the attached tubes.

Beginning to feel ill, Annie quickly closed the refrigerator door and left the kitchen. She walked into the dining room and weakly sat down on a chair at the big empty dining table, its rich oak surface dulled by dust.

Annie tried to pull herself together. It had never occurred to her that Rafael drank human blood. He'd told her that, while in wolf form, he attacked cattle for their blood. A fact which was unsettling enough, but she'd managed to put it out of her mind. Now to understand that he also needed human blood . . . well, that was much more to take in. She knew he was a vampire, of course, but the horrific details of his existence were only now becoming clear.

Where did he get the blood bags? Did he rob a hospital or blood bank? Or was he able to purchase them legally somehow?

"Don't think about it," she whispered to herself.

She looked around the empty dining room with its tall, draped windows and the large Navaho rug that covered most of the tiled floor. What should she do?

She was alone, no food, her only clothes the nightgown and bedroom slippers she had on. Annie still had her condo in Tucson, but with her truck left at the Logan ranch, she had no transportation. And then she remembered Inez had promised she'd bring Annie her things, all the belongings she'd left behind in her room at the Logan house.

Feeling stronger, Annie rose from the chair and walked into the living room, furnished with a tan leather couch and matching easy chairs. She'd seen this room many times on her nocturnal assignations with Rafael. The room was carpeted, there were floor lamps and a fireplace, whose marble mantle was dust free, as were the oak end tables and the low table in front of the couch. Oil paintings of scenic places in Spain decorated the walls. An old television stood in one corner. Rafael took care that this room should look homey and lived-in for visitors. He'd told her it was here that he met with his ranch foreman and his horse trainer in the evening to discuss business. A small room off of the living room served as his office, complete with a desk, file cabinets and a computer.

All at once Annie heard a vehicle coming up the gravel driveway. She peeked out the window and saw Inez pulling up to the front door in Annie's white Chevy pickup truck. Annie hurried to the entry hall to open the door for her. She watched as Inez, whose heritage was Mexican and Pueblo Indian, got out from behind the wheel. Inez wore a long denim skirt with a blouse and blue cardigan sweater. Her long gray hair hung in a thick braid down her back.

Inez walked to the passenger side, opened the door and pulled out a pile of clothes.

Annie stepped outside, glancing around to be sure there was no one to see her in her nightgown, and took some of the clothes from Inez. "Looks like you got everything," she said, quickly checking her pairs of jeans and khaki pants, shirts and sweaters. "Thanks *so* much, Inez."

"Your suitcase was up on the closet shelf. Too high for me. So I just grabbed the clothes. Brought this, too," Inez said, reaching in the truck. She pulled out a cream-colored silk suit on a hanger and wrapped in a clear plastic sheath.

Annie nodded reluctantly. The suit was to have served as her wedding attire. "I don't know when I'll ever wear it, but it was tailored to fit me, so I don't think I can return it."

They walked into the house together and dropped the clothes onto the couch. One of the sweaters got caught on Annie's left hand. She unhooked the clinging yarn and realized she was still wearing her engagement ring.

"Oh, no," Annie sighed. "I never thought about the diamond Brent gave me."

"Do you want me to take it and set it on the desk in your room?" Inez asked, hesitantly.

Annie shook her head. "I should return it in person. I feel bad enough that I only scribbled him a note saying I couldn't go through with the wedding. Leaving the ring would seem heartless. I'll wait a few days and visit Brent. I owe him that much."

Inez quietly nodded in agreement. She stepped back to the front door. "I also brought your backpack, your field notebook, and your purse and cell phone. And the artifacts from the ruin, the woven sandal you found and the potsherds."

Annie followed her outside to help. "It was Rafael who found the sandal. He'd shapeshifted to wolf form and brought it to me, carrying it in his mouth." She chuckled at the memory. "That was before he'd revealed himself to me as a man."

Annie felt free to talk, because Inez had told Annie her story. Rafael had come upon Inez when she was only nineteen as she watched the sunset alone at the ancient ruin. She'd allowed him to seduce her and then he had taken her blood, putting her under his power to keep her quiet about who and what he was. Inez had confided that through the supernatural bond he'd formed with her, he'd mentally called her to visit him in the night for thirty years, until she'd finally asked him to let her go.

Having heard Inez's long history with Rafael, Annie had understood why Inez could easily guess the reason Annie was sneaking off in the middle of the night. Inez seemed to accept that Annie and

Rafael had truly fallen in love, that his vampire powers had not forced their relationship.

Still, Annie felt the poignancy of Inez's situation. Now in her mid-sixties, Inez had never married and had no family, having lost her childbearing decades to Rafael. Inez's experience had given Annie reason to choose to marry Brent, who'd fallen for her. Though at times insensitive and controlling, he could nevertheless have given her a conventional life.

The two women carried everything into the living room. Inez held up a shopping bag.

"I brought you some food—eggs, bread, some canned stew."

"Thank you," Annie said with relief. "I checked Rafael's refrigerator, and . . . all I found were blood bags. I didn't know he needed human blood."

Inez nodded solemnly. "He would feed from me sometimes. In the old days."

"No . . . ," Annie said, shocked. "He did?"

"Yes. It kept the marks on my neck fresh, and I wore a bandana all those years to cover the wounds. It may sound odd, but I didn't mind."

"Because you were under his power?"

Inez took a moment, apparently mulling over the question. "Maybe. Still, I cared for him. He told me that animal blood can sustain him, but human blood gave him greater strength. And I wanted him to be strong." She shook her head thoughtfully. "That was so long ago. It's hard to believe now, that I had such an unbreakable bond with him."

"Is it uncomfortable for you to be here?" Annie asked.

Inez glanced around the room. "A little. But I'm happy for you. He loves you so much, he never took your blood. He was fond of me, and under his power I had no choice but to please him. You challenge him. I think he admires that. I don't believe in looking back, in being resentful. It's true, he took advantage of me. I had a special, secret relationship with him—and God forgive me, I enjoyed it. I'm older now. Life is different. Habit replaces happiness."

Habit replaces happiness. It struck Annie as a wistful statement. She was relieved that Inez seemed at peace with the past. But she wished Inez could say she was happy.

"Rafael told me there's an Indian shaman who could cure him of being a vampire," Annie said. "He told me he was willing to go to this shaman to become a mortal again, so he and I could have a normal life together. I don't know if I should agree, or if I should ask him to make me what he is. Otherwise, I'll grow old and he won't. Exactly what happened to you, Inez."

"I brought him to the shaman, Joe Strongwalker," Inez replied. "But after they met, I feared Rafael wouldn't survive the healing ritual. Restoring his life force sounded so mystical. Joe described it as a fragile, touch and go process. I talked Rafael out of it."

Inez sighed, sadness in her eyes. "Rafael was reluctant to perform the blood ceremony to make me a vampire, and my religious belief wouldn't allow me to ask it of him. My relationship with him was sinful enough. He understood my deep worry about my immortal soul, a burden that grew as I aged. He let me go just before I turned fifty. I can't tell you what to do, Annie. Life, death, immortality—these are questions we all grapple with. I put faith in the Catholic religion. But you must decide what's best for you. When a woman encounters a vampire, these questions become so much more real, don't they?"

"Yes, they do." Annie couldn't help her curiosity. "When he fed from you, did the blood loss leave you weak?"

Inez lifted her shoulders. "He was careful not to take too much. A person would lose more donating at a blood drive. Rafael is capable of savagery. But he was always gentle with me. I enjoyed giving him sustenance." She sighed and looked at Annie, urgency in her brown eyes. "I need to get back to the ranch before anyone misses me."

Savagery? Annie had to let the disturbing word go as she remembered that Inez had come in Annie's truck. "Yes, of course. I'll drive you."

"Someone might see," Inez argued. "Several of Brent's ranch hands get up at dawn."

"If they saw me drop you off, they'd figure out you helped me," Annie agreed, thinking it through. "Is there a truck here on Rafael's property you could borrow?"

Inez paused. "Maybe." She went to the front door, still open, and looked outside. She perked up. "There's Francisco. I'll ask him to drive me back."

"Who's Francisco?" Annie went to the door to see.

"I suppose you wouldn't have met him," Inez said. "Francisco Santos. He's been Rafael's horse trainer for many, many years. Long ago, he drove me home once. I'd come on horseback to be with Rafael, and the horse got loose and ran off. I hope Francisco doesn't remember that. I was very young then. So was he. I had black hair and smooth skin, no wrinkles. He'll never recognize me as that embarrassed girl who had obviously spent the night with his boss."

Annie saw a white-haired man wearing jeans and a denim jacket walking away from a duplex-style cottage a short distance off to the side of Rafael's house. Behind it stood the bunkhouse.

"What excuse will you give for being here now?" Annie asked, worried for Inez.

Inez seemed perplexed. Then she said, "I'm an old woman. I don't have to have a reason. I'll say I need a ride to the Logan ranch, that's all. Francisco knows I work there. Lately I've noticed him attending

Mass. He happened to sit next to me, and we talked a little. He told me he's started coming to church again since his wife died."

"You better hurry," Annie said, growing increasingly concerned. "It's well past dawn. We don't want Brent coming down for breakfast on his wedding day and finding you not there. There'll be enough of a frenzy when they discover the bride's gone missing."

Chapter Two

Inez left Annie at the door of Rafael's ranch house and walked toward Francisco, who was heading to the corral. He paused when he saw her approaching.

She felt a little nervous, but made an effort to look relaxed. "Francisco, how are you?"

"Fine, thanks, Inez. You?" He smiled, but looked a bit puzzled.

"Good. Say, do you have time to drive me back to the Logan ranch?"

"Well, sure. Be happy to." He glanced over her shoulder, and she knew he must be noticing the white pickup parked in front of Rafael's house. "Your truck broke down?"

"It's not mine."

His dark brown eyes seemed mystified. "How did you get here?"

"Long story," Inez said in a breezy tone. "Can we leave now? I really need to get back."

"My truck's over here." He pointed and they began to head toward a red pickup at the side of the duplex cottage he'd walked out of. "There's a wedding at the Logans' today, right? Brent's getting married. Saw the write-up in the newspaper."

"That's the plan." Inez kept her tone light. "You can see why I'm in a hurry."

"Doing the cooking?"

"No, it'll be catered," she replied as they reached his truck. "But they'll be needing me."

Francisco opened the passenger door for her and offered his hand to help Inez climb in. She smiled and thanked him. Though his hands were calloused and his face weathered from working outdoors all his life, he had a kind, gentlemanly quality that she appreciated. Brent Logan's cattle wranglers were polite and friendly, but they mostly treated her like a hired cook, which was what her job at the ranch had been for over forty-five years. Perhaps because Francisco had gained the reputation of being something of a horse-whisperer, with an instinctive understanding of the Appaloosas he trained, he seemed unusually sensitive to people, too. It was a rare trait, and Inez felt quite secure with Francisco.

He got behind the wheel and started the engine, then headed his pickup down the long gravel driveway toward the main road.

"Nice day for a wedding," he said in a cheerful tone.

"It is," Inez agreed, feeling uncomfortable keeping the secret that the wedding would not take place. She decided to change the subject. "How many Appaloosas are you training now?"

"A dozen foals were born in the spring. And we have a bunch of yearlings. Keeps me busy. How are things at the Logan spread? I saw Charlie at the saddle shop a few months ago."

Charlie Callahan was one of Brent's employees, the one who handled the horses used for herding cattle.

"Everyone's healthy. Doing well." Inez wished they could avoid talking about the Logan Ranch. She hoped her nervous impatience didn't show in her voice.

But maybe it had. Francisco grew quiet, perhaps sensing something was bothering her.

"You have children, don't you?" Inez tried to aim for pleasant chit-chat. "I recall at church you mentioned a son and daughter. Any grandchildren?"

He nodded. "My son lives in Phoenix with his wife and they have two boys. My daughter and her husband used to live next to me in the duplex, but he got a good job and they moved to Tucson. She's going to have their first child in June."

"Nice you have a growing family."

"What about you, Inez? Did you ever marry?"

The question took her off guard. She didn't like to talk about herself. In fact, she avoided it with everyone, except lately, when she confided in Annie. Why was he asking if she *ever* married? On the rare occasion when someone new asked her about herself, they usually wondered if she had grandchildren, having assumed she'd followed the usual route of wedlock and children. Francisco's inserting the word *ever* in his question made it sound as if he might know something he shouldn't. Did he remember driving her home after she'd spent the night with Rafael all those decades ago? But if he did, wouldn't Rafael have used his mind control to make Francisco forget? Rafael could mentally manipulate men without taking their blood. It didn't work with women, however.

Inez drew a long breath and feigned a smile. "I never married."

"Hmm." A twinkle appeared in Francisco's eye. "Then some dumb guy missed the boat. A nice-looking woman like you, and a good cook to boot. You'd be a great wife."

Inez took in his words with silent astonishment. Nice looking? She was short, had gray hair and hands gnarled with arthritis. Wrinkles crinkled around her mouth and brown eyes. She saw them every time she looked in a mirror, which she avoided doing as much as possible.

And then it occurred to her. Was Francisco, well . . . *flirting* with her? *No . . . why would he?* But his wife had died a few years ago. And he had chosen to sit next to Inez at Mass more than once, when there was plenty of space in other pews. When they rose from kneeling, he'd taken her arm to assist her. *Holy Mother of God . . . .*

Relief struck her when she looked out the window and saw the Logan house in the distance. "Oh, we're here! You can let me out. I'll walk the rest of the way."

"No, I'll drive you to the door," Francisco said.

Inez worried someone might see her being dropped off. "No, please. This is far enough. I prefer to walk the rest of the way."

Francisco seemed troubled, but he slowed the truck to a stop at the end of the long driveway to the house. He got out of the driver's seat and walked around the front fender to help Inez step down from the truck. Just then another pickup truck passed them, slowing to turn down the driveway toward the house. The driver, a middle-aged, round-faced man, stopped and waved.

"Hey, Francisco."

Francisco waved back. "Charlie! How are you?"

"Can't complain." Charlie looked at her with curiosity. "Hey, Inez."

Inez recognized Charlie with alarm. This was exactly what she didn't want to happen. He lived in town and was coming in early today. And no doubt he was wondering where she'd been and why she was with Francisco.

"Hello," she said, trying to sound nonchalant.

"Want a ride up to the house?" Charlie asked, a nosey light in his eyes.

"No, thanks."

Charlie waved again with a smile and drove off.

Inez turned to Francisco. "Thank you so much."

"You're welcome. Sure I can't take you to the door?"

"No," she said with impatience. Suddenly men were being so helpful. It was annoying!

"Okay," Francisco acquiesced. "See you at Mass maybe."

"Sure, sure. Bye." Inez headed toward the house, ruffled and perturbed. And worried. She hoped Brent would not hear that she'd been seen being dropped off by Francisco, as that could lead to questions she didn't want to answer. At least no one knew that Annie had run off with Rafael, so Annie's connection to Rancho de la Noche could not be made. Yet.

# # #

A half-hour later, Inez stood at the cooktop in the Logan kitchen, with its granite countertops and terra-cotta-tiled floor, making scrambled eggs with cream cheese, bacon, and waffles. So far she hadn't seen Brent or Zoe, his sixteen-year-old daughter, but it was nearing seven a.m., the time they usually came down for breakfast. Inez cooked for them as well as for the employees who lived on the property. She wondered if Charlie would eat with the ranch hands today, since he'd come to work early.

All at once Brent burst into the kitchen, casually dressed and full of energy, a grin on his face. A handsome man of forty-eight with graying black hair, his blue eyes brimmed with excitement. "Morning, Inez. Annie up yet?"

Inez lifted her shoulders, as if to say, *I don't know*. She didn't like to lie, and hoped if she managed not to verbally reply, she would feel less guilty. "Breakfast is ready. I'll bring it into the dining room."

"Okay. Zoe is at the table already. Annie should be up soon." He left the kitchen.

After Inez had served Brent and Zoe, she placed the rest of the prepared food on a two-tiered metal cart that she wheeled down a short walkway to the rustic bunkhouse dining room. She served the men waiting there.

Charlie sat with the others and eyed Inez mischievously as she placed the serving dishes on the big, round table. "You and Francisco have a little romance going?"

Inez turned on him, appalled. "Of course not. I hardly know him."

"But he drove you home this morning," Charlie countered with practical logic.

"That's . . . a long story," Inez said. "Nothing romantic! I'm past all that."

"Why?" Charlie asked. "I always hoped you had some fun in your life, besides cookin' all day."

The other half dozen men were eyeing her curiously, obviously wondering what the conversation was all about.

"Eat," she told them. "Before it gets cold." And then she left, knowing they'd be gossiping about her.

No time to think about that now. The fat would hit the fan any minute.

She entered the back door of the house to find Brent in the hallway, knocking on the door to the room Annie had been staying in, next to Inez's room.

"Annie," Brent called brightly. "Breakfast is ready. Lots to do—it's our wedding day."

Inez chewed her lip nervously as she walked into the kitchen, the door to which lay directly across the short hallway from her bedroom and Annie's. She found her hands were shaking a bit over the sink as she began to scrub a frying pan.

"Annie!" Brent called again. "What the . . . ?"

Inez heard him open the door. She stopped scrubbing and closed her eyes, imagining him finding the room empty and a note for him on the desk. Already she felt sorry for him. He might not have made the best husband for Annie, but Inez knew he'd fallen for her.

"Inez!"

She jumped at Brent's voice. He rushed into the kitchen, waving Annie's penciled note in his hand.

"Look at this! She ran out on me! Did you know?"

"She didn't say anything last evening," Inez told him truthfully.

Brent eyed her. "You don't seem surprised."

Inez understood that she should be feigning astonishment, but knew she was a lousy actress.

"Annie . . . confided to me that she had doubts. But when she went to bed she seemed committed to being your bride. I'm so sorry, Brent."

"Do you know where she went?"

"Why w-would I know anything?" Inez improvised.

"You said she confided in you."

Inez decided to take a matronly tone. After all, she'd watched him grow up from the time he was a toddler. "Brent, if she's made the decision not to go through with the wedding, then you must respect that."

"Not going through with the wedding?" Zoe repeated with surprise as she entered the kitchen wearing jeans and a snug T-shirt. Her short blond hair had a streak of fuchsia. "What do you mean?"

Brent hesitated, then showed his daughter Annie's note. "You might as well see it for yourself."

"'I'm sorry, Brent, I can't go through with the wedding. I wish you well. Goodbye,'" Zoe read with dismay. "So . . . she just left? During the night?"

"Snuck off like a thief." Brent's voice seethed with anger. "Too much of a coward to tell me in person."

Zoe gave him a reprimanding look. "You're so controlling, I can't blame her."

Brent's face reddened. "What?"

"You decided when the wedding would be. You arranged the whole honeymoon without asking her.

You didn't like her continuing her career. You were pulling all the same stuff you did on Mom. Maybe Annie was smart enough to see that she wouldn't be happy. The wedding day probably made everything real. She left in secret so you couldn't talk her into staying."

As if he could, Inez thought. She continued washing pans while Brent lit into a tirade at Zoe. She glanced over her shoulder and saw the petulant teen withstand his rage with a defiant look on her face. Inez wished she had that much self-assurance, but she hadn't been a rich man's daughter.

Born to a poor family in Laguna Pueblo, New Mexico, Inez had always felt fortunate to have a life-long job as the Logan cook. Her aunt had used to be their cook and had recommended they take on Inez when Inez was only eighteen. She moved to Arizona with her parent's approval. The job provided her a living and a place in the world, a secure future and even a bit of status for an impoverished Mexican-Indian girl. At nineteen, she'd encountered Rafael, who had sealed her fate in a different way. Now, with few close relatives left, all she had was her job and her modest life savings.

"Instead of yelling at me," Zoe was telling her father, "why don't you start figuring out what to do about the cancelled wedding? Guests will be showing up. The ceremony was supposed to be at four, and what about the catered dinner? Do we call everyone and tell them not to come?"

Brent stared at her, fuming. "It's too hard to get in touch with everyone. The caterers have already been paid. Let it be. I'll show Annie. We'll just go ahead and have the best party ever. Celebrate that I escaped a close call and almost married the wrong girl!"

"Woman, Dad. Annie's a grown woman with a mind of her own. You never quite got that. In a few years, I'll be eighteen. You better get it through your head that you won't be able to push me around anymore, either."

"Go to your room!"

Zoe stood her ground. "Can't. It's my job to greet the flower people and show them where the arrangements should be placed."

"Damn it all to hell!" Brent exclaimed and stormed out of the kitchen.

Inez breathed a long sigh of relief that the arguing was over. She turned to Zoe. "You know you shouldn't talk to your father that way. But I agree with you."

Zoe nodded, and Inez was surprised to see tears welling in the girl's blue eyes.

"I don't blame Annie for running out on my dad, but I wish I'd had a chance to say goodbye. I was starting to really like her."

Inez dried her wet hands on a dish towel and gave Zoe a hug. "I like Annie, too."

Zoe sniffed. "Do you know where she went?"

Inez hesitated and looked away.

"You know, but you can't say," Zoe surmised.

"Don't tell your father, but yes, I know."

"Will I be able to see her again someday?"

Inez nodded. "She means to talk to Brent and give him back the engagement ring. I'm sure she would like to see you, too. There's hope you can stay friends with her. Though that depends on your father."

"Never mind him," Zoe said, matter-of-factly. "I'll find a way, whether he likes it or not."

Inez smiled, knowing Zoe would indeed figure out a way. After all, Inez had successfully kept her trysts with Rafael a secret from the Logan family.

Fortunately, Annie could be a positive influence on Zoe's life. Rafael, by contrast, had given Inez years of intense passion she would never have found with an ordinary man—but it was an unholy relationship. With him she'd shared decades of sin. She knew God had forgiven her. But she was alone.

Inez couldn't help but wonder, what would Annie's future be?

Chapter Three

Rafael awoke from his lethargy, and his first thought was, *Is Annie still here?*

He lifted the lid of the coffin, got to his feet and stepped out. After extinguishing the burned down candle with his fingertips, he climbed the stairs in the dark, apprehension in his heart. He entered the unlit kitchen and hurried through the empty dining room. His spirit soared when he saw the lights on in the living room.

"Annie?"

"I'm here." She quickly appeared in the wide doorway between the dining room and living room.

Smiling, Annie ran up to him and they embraced.

"I was afraid you'd change your mind," he said, his lips against her forehead. He knelt in front of her, his cheek pressing into the soft chambray shirt covering her chest, where he could hear her heartbeat. He clung to her in adoration. "Thank you for staying."

Annie bent over him. "Of course I stayed. I told you, I love you too much to ever leave you."

He rose to his feet and beheld her. "My beautiful soul mate. Strange that we were born centuries and continents apart, yet fate brought us together. I love you as I've never loved anyone." He stroked her long hair. "You're dressed. Inez did as she promised and brought over your things?"

"Yes. There was room in the closet in your bedroom, so I hung my clothes in there."

This reassured him a great deal. "So you've truly moved in. We're really living together."

Annie grinned. "We absolutely are."

He leaned against the doorframe. "I wish you and I could be married." His earnest emotion colored his voice. "But I'm not sure how that would be possible. Being what I am, I don't think I can darken the door of a church. I sense that God has turned away from me. My legal status is precarious. I don't have a birth certificate or even a driver's license. Perhaps I could have them forged, like I did my social security number half a century ago. Ben Franklin said nothing is certain except death and taxes. I may be cheating death, but I knew I'd better not mess with Uncle Sam."

Annie chuckled. "I don't care if we're married." She raised her delicate eyebrows. "I wonder what's happening at the Logan Ranch. They were supposed to be serving the wedding cake about now. I can only imagine their confusion this morning when they discovered I'd run off. Brent was probably furious. And Zoe . . . I think I feel more regret about leaving Zoe than any guilt about Brent. Zoe and I were beginning to hit it off. Brent doesn't know how to handle her, and she was actually starting to listen to me."

Rafael had never met Zoe, but Annie's tender concern for the girl touched him. "Maybe Inez will be able to comfort her."

"Maybe." Annie looked at Rafael, worry in her eyes. "Inez didn't want me to drive her back to the ranch. Afraid someone might see. So she asked Francisco. I haven't met him yet. I watched him drive her away, and he seemed nice enough about it. But do you think Francisco might be wondering what she was doing here?"

Rafael paused a moment, thinking. "Francisco is discreet. If he's noticed that I haven't aged, he doesn't say. Years ago, I could make him forget questions that arose in his mind about me, or things he shouldn't have seen. But the last decade or so, I notice that he avoids looking me in the eye, and I think it's because he senses I can interfere with his thoughts. I do it through eye contact, you see." Rafael tilted his head. "His way of training horses is so valuable and unique, I depend on him. In fact, I worry that he's aging. And sometimes I worry what he may suspect about me, the fact that I'm only out at night and I look the same as the evening long ago that he first applied to work for me."

"So you won't be able to make him forget driving Inez home," Annie surmised.

Rafael shook his head. "Any of my other men, I could. But not Francisco, not anymore. Yet, I think we can trust him not to say anything. He's a quiet man, not given to gossip."

"What about me living here with you?" Annie asked. "What will you tell him?"

Rafael smiled. "I'll just have to introduce you as my ladylove, my companion. It'll be something new. I've never openly lived with a woman before. My past relationships all happened in secret."

Annie seemed composed as she took this in. He revered her for accepting who and what he was, for knowing his long history with women, including Inez, and being willing to overlook it.

She gazed up at him. "I'll be happy to meet Francisco. I'm glad he'll know I'm here and that we'll be straightforward about it all. Because he may put it together that I'm the same woman who jilted Brent. Brent had an engagement announcement with our photo put in the newspaper, including the wedding date. We weren't engaged long, so the announcement appeared only a few weeks ago."

"I suppose more may be revealed than we would wish," Rafael agreed. He didn't like attention drawn to himself. But this couldn't be helped. "If we just move on quietly, any whiff of scandal will soon pass."

Annie drew away a bit and bowed her head. Then she looked up at him tentatively and lifted her left hand. "Rafael, I forgot to leave behind my engagement ring."

The large diamond sparkled brightly, annoying him. "Why are you still wearing it?"

"It cost a small fortune. I didn't want to misplace it," she explained. "I need to return it to Brent. And I think I should do it in person. He deserves his ring back and an explanation."

Rafael looked away, disconcerted, worried for her well-being. "I don't like you seeing him."

"I know. I'm not looking forward to it. He'll be hurt and angry. He has a temper."

Alarmed, Rafael said, "Should I come with you?"

"That wouldn't be a good idea. I'll be all right." She hesitated. "How much should I tell him? I suppose he'll find out I'm with you. Your ranch hands will see me here. Even you can't make everyone forget."

Rafael pondered his options. There weren't many. "Then tell him the truth. Leaving out the fact that you forsook him for a vampire."

She laughed, lights in her eyes, which pleased him. "Who would believe that? For all Brent knows, you're an old-timer. I may have to say that you're a descendant of the first Rafael de la Vega. Would that be all right?"

He pulled her against him and lowered his head so that his nose touched hers. "Okay. You're sure you won't see Logan and wish you'd married him? You must have found him attractive enough to let him put that rock on your finger."

She unbuttoned his shirt and slid her hands underneath. "No mortal man compares to you," she whispered. "I'm completely under your spell." She smiled. "I've been waiting all day for you, Rafael." She unbuttoned her own shirt, revealing her round, perfect breasts and pink, hardening nipples. "Didn't bother with undies. Saves time."

With both hands he caressed her breasts, finding their feminine softness comforting. His thumbs teased her upturned nipples. Thoroughly aroused, he pressed his groin against her pelvis. She drew in a long, quivering breath and her eyes brightened with excitement as she leaned into the hardness beneath his zipper.

"Let's go to the bedroom." Her voice had grown husky with desire.

He picked her up in his arms and carried her to his big bed. In moments they'd torn off their clothes. She lay on the quilt bedspread beneath him, breathing hard as she parted her thighs for him. He slid into her gently and watched her close her eyes with pleasure. As he began back and forth thrusts, her face became a picture of erotic euphoria.

"Rafael, Rafael. No one is like you." Her voice was breathy, interspersed with gasps and moans of delight. "Ohh, yes. More . . . more. Ohh . . ."

With joy and adoration, he gave her all she wanted, reveling in her cries of ecstasy as her body throbbed with orgasm after orgasm, while his engorged hardness pulsed with powerful fulfillment inside her quaking body.

Afterward she lay limply in his arms. "You've absolutely spoiled me for anyone else," she said, touching his face. "I could never want any other man."

"That's good to know." He smiled at her. "Because I want to love you this way forever."

He stroked her breasts, still firm and swollen from his fondling and her arousal. With renewed anticipation he watched her nipples peak again. Bending over her, he kissed each pert nipple ardently, careful not to nick her tender skin with his sharp incisors. She breathed deeply and writhed in response.

He lifted his head. "Ready for more? I am."

Her small, feminine hands took hold of his enlarging member, increasing his urgency. "You're so endlessly virile. You wear me out," she cooed with delight as she guided him into her hot, eager body again. He resumed long, slow, sensual thrusts, the way he knew she liked it. Taking his time, he brought her to even more ecstatic heights that made her cry out, as if for mercy. But she clearly did not want to stop. Soon her body broke into tight spasms around his member, giving him such intense pleasure he thought he might perish of joy.

Afterward, they lay together in each other's arms, all problems forgotten in their bliss.

#

Brent's cheeks hurt from forcing himself to smile. From the time wedding guests, mostly his relatives and friends, began to arrive until now, as he sat at the table next to Zoe, he'd put on what he thought was a masterful performance. He portrayed a man who'd been jilted at the altar with humor and aplomb.

At four p.m. when the ceremony was to take place, he'd stood up in front of the one hundred invited guests, alongside the judge who was to perform the ceremony, and said, "Folks, here's the news. My bride went AWOL. So let's celebrate my unexpected new freedom! We're passing out glasses of champagne. In a while we'll serve an excellent dinner. Let's party!"

Some gasps had been heard at first, but the guests went along with his devil-may-care attitude, drank their champagne and soon were enjoying a convivial atmosphere. Brent had kept moving, greeting people, avoiding lengthy conversations about the reasons the wedding had been cancelled. The most he revealed was, "She left a note saying she couldn't go through with it. That's all I know. And all I need to know. I'll never take her back."

Now, as the caterers began passing out pieces of wedding cake for dessert, Brent found he couldn't keep up his front a minute longer. He quietly got up and left the poolside where the tables and chairs, covered in white satin, were set up along with heat lamps to stave off the evening chill. He went to his bedroom and closed the door. Sinking down on the bed, head in hands, he found tears streaming down his cheeks.

"Damn her," he muttered, wiping away the wetness with his fingers. His tears embarrassed him. Mature men didn't bawl like babies.

He recalled what Zoe had told him when he first found Annie's note. Maybe he was too autocratic. Even controlling. He had to be to keep his cattle ranch running and profitable. But he remembered Annie didn't like it when he tried to tell her how she should wear her hair for the wedding. Stupid of him. What did he know about hair anyway?

Maybe Annie had her reasons. But did she have to run off in the night, leaving him a scribbled note? Couldn't she have faced him and told him, not just disappeared? He wouldn't have believed it of her, that she would do this. Still couldn't believe it. Where did she go? To her condo in Tucson? He'd tried to call her, but she wasn't answering her cell phone.

And what did Inez know that she wasn't saying? He'd seen that she and Annie had gotten to be good friends, which had pleased him. Inez's room was right next to the room Annie had been staying in while she excavated the Anasazi ruin. If Annie snuck off in the night, taking all her things, wouldn't Inez have heard some noise?

He knew Inez was a light sleeper. About eight months ago, when Zoe had tried to sneak away one night to meet a boy, Inez had heard her and awakened Brent. He'd had no idea what his daughter was up to. If she'd heard Zoe trying to slip out the back door of the ranch house, wouldn't she have heard Annie?

Brent chastened himself. He shouldn't accuse Inez of anything without proof. She'd been loyal to the Logan family all her adult life. He'd thought Annie was loyal to him, too. Not very bright on his part. How long had he known Annie? Six or seven months? Obviously not enough time. He'd married Inger too quickly, too. Of course, Inger had been pregnant with Zoe, so he had to do the right thing.

He needed to try to understand women better. That's what he ought to learn from this fiasco. He was too vulnerable around them. Maybe he shouldn't even want to be married. Being a bachelor had its lonely moments, and he sure could use a stepmom for Zoe. But if women were this much trouble, then maybe he should just stay single.

The old movie of *My Fair Lady* came to mind. Inger had wanted to see it years ago, so they'd rented the DVD. He recalled Rex Harrison singing about how irrational women were. That their heads were filled with cotton and rags. That about summed it up!

Chapter Four

The next day, feeling tired, angry and depressed, Brent made an effort to go on with work at the ranch as if nothing had happened. He decided some mundane task would be best. He headed to the stables to get his horse, Sunny, to ride the fences along his property to look for any damage. He ran into Charlie there, examining the horseshoe on the hind leg of another horse.

"Hey, Charlie." Brent tried to sound upbeat.

Charlie looked up. "Hey, Brent." Usually talkative, Charlie seemed to hesitate over what to say next.

"Loose shoe?" Brent asked.

"Yeah. Milky Way will be good to go in a little while." He patted the white horse's rump. "Um . . . too bad about . . ."

"No need to talk about it," Brent said. "Today's a new day. Who needs a wife? You're a happy bachelor, aren't you, Charlie?"

"Yup. Had a wife once. Been there, done that. Talk about disasters!" He laughed heartily.

After a moment's pause, Charlie came around Milky Way's backside, his chin raised to indicate he had something to tell Brent.

"Say, here's a curious thing. Early yesterday morning, I saw Francisco you know, from Rancho de la Noche—drop off Inez. Way down where our

driveway meets the main road. I saw them, slowed
my truck to say hey, and even offered to take Inez to
the house. But she said no. She walked to the house
instead. Like maybe she didn't want anyone to see
her. At breakfast I joked that she must be having a
romance with Francisco, and she hotly denied it. But
what was she doing with him at six-thirty in the a.m.?
Looks to me like those two are getting a little nooky."

Brent listened with increasing interest. "You're
right, that *is* curious. But that's not like Inez to . . . oh,
no, she's very religious. Goes to Mass every Sunday.
I've never known her to be involved with any man."

"That's what I thought, too. When she got
insulted, I told her I hoped she had some fun besides
cookin' all day."

Brent looked at Charlie and nodded, though he
didn't exactly like Charlie's statement. Brent had
always assumed Inez was content with her life and
happy to be working for the Logan family. When she
was younger, she sometimes seemed really tired and
he wondered if her job was too much for her. But the
last fifteen years or so, she seemed to have more
energy and accomplished a lot, even though she'd
developed some arthritis.

So . . . why did Francisco drive Inez home, just in
time so she could prepare breakfast? Where had she
met up with him? At de la Vega's ranch? Why would
she have gone there? Especially the night before the
wedding was to take place. Brent couldn't help but

wonder if there was some connection between Inez's unusual behavior and Annie's disappearance.

"Thanks for telling me, Charlie."

"Sure. Glad I happened to drive by them just then."

Instead of taking Sunny out of the stall, Brent changed his mind about riding the fences and went back to the house.

# # #

Inez was cleaning the kitchen cooktop burners when Brent came through the door. He poured himself a mug of leftover breakfast coffee and took a sip.

"How are you doing, Inez?" Brent set the cup down and leaned against the granite counter a few feet from her.

She noticed the cool tone in his voice. "Good, thanks. And you?"

"How do you think? Being left at the altar isn't the most cheering thing I've ever had happen."

"I'm sure it isn't," Inez said with genuine sympathy. "I'm so sorry about it all."

"Are you?"

She turned to stare at him. "Of course. I know you were fond of Annie."

"I'd rather not hear her name. Just tell me, did you have anything to do with helping her leave? Her truck and all her things are gone. Poof, just like that. Did she do that all by herself?"

Inez swallowed. "Why would you think I helped?"

"I heard from Charlie that Francisco Santos dropped you off up by the highway early yesterday. Why were you with him?"

She turned her attention back to cleaning the stove. "That's a private matter."

"You and Francisco are having an affair?" Brent asked.

"No," Inez said with a sharp sigh. She felt the weight of guilt settling on her shoulders. This wasn't a secret she could keep. She didn't like to lie. If only Charlie hadn't seen them.

"What are you hiding, Inez?"

After a long, anxious pause, Inez knew she couldn't withhold the truth from Brent. He'd find out eventually.

"All right. I did help Annie. She made the decision not to marry you and left. I brought her things to her in her truck. I had no way to get back, so I called on Francisco, who was kind enough to drive me. I asked him to drop me off at the highway, hoping no one would see. But Charlie did, and there you have it."

"She left? How? Why did she leave her truck behind?"

Inez looked up at the ceiling. "Someone came for her."

"Who?"

Inez went back to cleaning and did not reply.

"Keeping mum, eh?" Brent's tone grew increasingly sharp. "If you brought her stuff to her, you must know where she is."

Inez closed her eyes. "Yes."

"Where? Rancho de la Noche?"

She opened her eyes and looked at him squarely. "I won't tell you. It's for her to decide what she wants to reveal. She's planning to see you to return the diamond ring."

Brent's head went back in surprise. "She is? When?"

"I don't know."

He breathed deeply, looking startled and confused. "I didn't think I'd see her again. I don't want to. She can keep the damn ring."

"She said she feels she owes you an explanation," Inez said, gently.

"Explanation!" Brent picked up his mug from the counter and threw it onto the tile floor, where it noisily smashed into pieces in an expanding puddle of coffee. "How the hell can she explain leaving me flat and embarrassed on our wedding day? Huh? There is no explanation. And you, helping her. I never thought you would be so disloyal, after I and my family have been so good to you all these years."

His words struck Inez in the heart. She took a step backward. "You have been good to me. I never meant to be disloyal. It's just . . . Annie had changed her mind. She realized she was in love with someone else. He came for her, begged her to go away with him. And she did. It was a spur of the moment decision. All I did was bring over her things afterward. I tried to keep it quiet, but I see now that was a mistake. I'm sorry."

"She fell in love with some other guy?" Brent said, astonished. "And you knew?"

Inez rubbed her forehead with a shaky hand. "Only recently. I suspected something . . . but there was nothing I could do to stop her from falling for him. When he came for her, it was inevitable that she would go."

"Who is this guy?" Brent demanded.

"That's for her to say. I can't reveal who he is. I . . . simply can't." Though she was no longer under Rafael's power, their bond having ended over fifteen years ago, she still felt incapable of revealing anything that might somehow expose Rafael.

Brent stepped closer, towering over her. "I never imagined you, of all people, could be so secretive and false. Some other guy in my fiancée's life that you knew about, and you not only never said a word of warning to me, but you helped her desert me. That's it, Inez. I'm done with you. You're fired! Pack up your things and leave today."

"W-what?" Inez felt lightheaded and held onto the countertop. The gray granite felt cold beneath her fingers. "Who will cook for you and your men?"

"That's not your problem. Just leave!"

"I have no place to go."

"Too bad. Get my cheating runaway bride to return your favor and help you." With that, he stormed out of the kitchen.

Inez sat down at the small kitchen table, stunned, having trouble catching her breath. After several minutes, she got her cell phone out of her apron pocket and dialed Annie's number.

# # #

"He fired you?" Annie repeated, aghast, her face and hands suddenly feeling icy as she held her cell phone to her ear. "Oh, no, Inez. I'm so sorry."

"He wants me out of the house today," Inez said, tearfully, over the phone. "I have nowhere to go. I don't even have a car of my own. Always used one of the ranch trucks to buy groceries or go to Mass."

"You can come here," Annie reassured her. "I'll pick you up."

Inez hesitated before replying. "But . . . I don't know how Rafael would feel about that."

"Why would he mind?" Annie said.

"We have an unusual past, he and I." Inez seemed to choose her words carefully. "And now you're with him. It just seems awkward."

Annie thought a moment, understanding why Inez might feel uncomfortable. "Rafael would want to help you. I'm quite sure of that. It can just be temporary until you figure out what to do."

"Okay," Inez agreed with a regretful sigh. "Just so you know, when I told Brent you were going to give your ring back, he said he didn't want to see you. He was demanding explanations and I reluctantly told him you were in love with another man. Maybe you shouldn't come here. He was terribly angry. I could probably get one of the men to drive me to Rancho de la Noche."

"It's because of me you got fired," Annie said. "And even if he's angry, I still think I should see Brent in person. Try to explain, even if he won't listen. So here's what we'll do. You start packing up your things. I'll drive my truck over in two hours and help you load up everything. And I'll talk to Brent. Did he have any plans to go out today?"

"Not that I know of," Inez replied. "After all the hubbub yesterday, I doubt he wants to see anyone."

"Hubbub? What happened?" Annie asked.

"He announced to the guests that his bride went AWOL, as he put it. And then he said everyone should stay for dinner and celebrate his bachelorhood.

I noticed he left in the middle of dinner, though. People were whispering and gossiping."

"I see," Annie said quietly. She felt bad about the pain she'd caused Brent. "At least it's over now." Taking a positive tone, she added, "Don't worry about anything, Inez. Rafael and I will see to it that you are taken care of."

After Inez said goodbye, Annie sat still for a while, the cell phone in her hand. Looked like she'd be seeing Brent sooner than she'd thought. She'd hoped to let things cool down for at least a few days.

Annie wished she could consult Rafael about all this. She didn't think he'd mind Inez taking refuge with them, but in truth she wasn't quite sure how he'd react. It was still morning and Rafael wouldn't rise until sundown. Annie had no choice but to make some decisions in the meantime.

Chapter Five

A couple of hours later, dressed in pants, a blouse and sweater, Annie drove to the Logan Ranch. She'd given Inez a quick call. Inez had said she was nearly ready, and that Brent was home. A cold feeling of apprehension came over Annie as she parked at the back of the house. She still had a key, but found the rear door—through which she'd escaped with Rafael—was unlocked. Walking in, she found Inez's belongings piled in the hallway.

Inez came out of her room carrying a laptop computer and looking distraught. "Annie. Thank goodness." She held up the closed laptop. "Brent gave me this on my sixtieth birthday. Should I keep it or give it back?"

Annie shrugged. "That was several years ago. It was a gift. Why not keep it?"

"Well, I think he gave it to me so I could order supplies online for the ranch. Though I used it for personal things, too. Pinterest, and I email my brother and a few cousins in New Mexico."

"Keep it," Annie said. "It's probably getting outdated anyway."

Inez nodded. "I suppose so. Should I start loading my stuff in your pickup?" She peeked out the open back door.

"Sure, go ahead. I'll . . . go see Brent," Annie said with an apprehensive exhale. "Is he in his office?"

"I think so. But I haven't looked for him."

Annie left Inez and walked to the other end of the house, where Brent's office was located. She saw the open door and quietly looked in. Brent was sitting at his desk, scattered papers in front of him, but he didn't seem to be studying them. His eyes had a sullen, glazed appearance.

"Hello, Brent," Annie said as she tentatively stepped into the room.

He looked up, saw her, and his eyes flashed with hostility. "You have a lot of nerve entering my house. Get out."

Annie took the diamond ring out of her pants pocket and held it up. "I want to return this."

"Why? Out of guilt? Throw it in the trash. I don't want it."

She stepped closer. "It's a big diamond and worth a lot of money. You can sell it. Or have it made into a necklace for Zoe when she turns eighteen." She set the ring on the corner of his desk.

He made an expression of disgust, but did not object further. His blue eyes connected with hers, blazing with anger. "Inez says you dumped me for some other guy. Were you cheating on me? While we were engaged?"

Annie swallowed. "After I said yes to your proposal, I . . . I didn't cheat. I broke it off with him."

"But while you were here, and I was wooing you, you were with this other man? Having sex with him, while I was being a gentleman and waiting to marry you?"

What could she say but the blunt truth? "I wasn't looking for a relationship. It just happened. I met him unexpectedly and . . . we fell in love. I wanted to choose you, to have a settled life with you and Zoe, so I said yes. And I broke off with him. But early yesterday morning, before dawn, he came to my window and asked me not to marry you. He begged me to choose him. He's my soul mate, and I love him so much, I realized I had to go with him." Tears filled Annie's eyes. "I'm sorry, Brent. I never meant to hurt you, yet I know I have."

"Who is this guy? Do I know him? I'll ring his neck!"

Annie wiped away a tear and slowly shook her head. "You can't hurt him, Brent."

"You've wounded me, and you're protecting him? I'll beat the heck out of him!"

"You don't understand," she said with patience. "He'll demolish you. Don't even think about going after him. I'm saying this to protect *you*."

Brent laughed. "Oh ho! So he's a real two-fisted bruiser, is he? A dynamo in bed, too, I suppose. Who is this macho super-hunk?"

"You don't need to know who he is."

"Oh, yeah? I'll find out. You're obviously staying somewhere nearby—Inez brought you your stuff. And Francisco drove her back here." He paused, thinking. "You know, I assumed Inez had something going with Francisco. But maybe it's *you*. I've met him—Francisco looks like he's twenty years older than me, with his white hair and all. And you think I'm not capable of tearing his head off?"

Annie roughly shoved her bangs away from her forehead. "It's not Francisco. And stop talking about tearing anyone's head off."

"You're nothing to me anymore," Brent said in a harsh, hoarse voice. "You can't tell me what to do!"

"No. But I never thought you were a violent man, or I wouldn't have even considered marrying you."

Her statement seemed to give him pause. He shifted his position in his high-back leather chair and appeared to regroup. Maybe he did still care what she thought of him.

In a quieter tone, he said, "Okay, no violence. But who is your lover? I'd like to know just so I can avoid him."

Now that she'd moved into Rancho de la Noche, Annie knew he'd find out eventually. "It's Rafael de la Vega."

Brent's dark brows drew together. "What? You ran off with an aged recluse?"

"He's not aged. He looks like he's in his early thirties. Maybe a little reclusive, but he's extremely fit and agile, stronger than you can imagine."

Brent looked confused. "How can that be?"

"He's a grandson with the same name," she said, using the explanation Rafael had agreed to.

"I never heard de la Vega had a family. Nobody ever knew much about him. How did you meet him?"

"At the ruin. He loves the cliff dwelling and visits there. He didn't like my being there at first, but then . . . his attitude changed. We fell in love."

Brent chuckled in an unpleasant way. "Don't think you can continue excavating that ruin. *My* ruin. From now on, you, and de la Vega, will be looked upon as trespassers. I'll have my men check on the place. If you're found there, I'll prosecute you to the full extent of the law."

Shock ran through Annie's system. "But I need to finish my work."

"Tough. Should have thought of that before you jilted me for your secret lover."

She closed her eyes, thinking how she could convince him. "But you're not just hurting me. You're preventing important research. There's so much archeologists can learn from an unexcavated ruin about the Anasazi, their culture, why they abandoned their homes."

"Then you shouldn't have abandoned me," he said, blithely. He made a show of pushing the papers on his desk into a neat pile. "That's all. You've given me the ring. You can go."

"But--"

"Don't come back."

Annie could see from his unyielding tone and stiff posture that there was nothing more she could say that would change his mind. She turned and walked out, blinking back tears as she headed into the dining room. There she encountered Zoe. It was Sunday, so the teen was home from school, dressed in old jeans and a sweater.

"Hello, Zoe." She greeted the girl tentatively, not sure how Zoe would feel toward her.

"Annie," Zoe said with surprise. "Are you and Dad working things out?" she asked, hope in her voice.

Annie sadly shook her head. "No. I came to give him back the ring. And now he says he won't let me continue excavating the ruin. I don't know why I'm surprised. Should have expected that."

"Why did you leave? Because Dad was getting so highhanded with you? I don't blame you, but I thought if anyone could get him to see the light, it would be you. I was looking forward to the wedding. We'd be a complete family."

Annie opened her arms and gave Zoe a hug. "I think I regret leaving you more than anything else." She drew back. "I hope we can stay in touch."

"Are you going to live in Tucson in your condo?"

"I'll probably keep the condo, since I'm still going to teach at the university. But I'm living at Rancho de la Noche. The reason I left is because I fell in love—deeply in love—with Rafael de la Vega. I didn't intend for it to happen. I never meant to hurt your father. Or you. But I realized I couldn't marry Brent when I was so in love with someone else."

Zoe wrinkled her nose. "Rafael de la Vega? He's a really old guy."

Annie laughed. "I think he looks younger than me. And he loves me. Said he can't go on without me. I'm sorry about the cancelled wedding. It must have been awful for you."

Zoe nodded quietly. "It was. At first. But once they started serving the champagne, everyone perked up. The catered dinner was really good and the guests seemed happy enough. Except for Dad. He disappeared into his room. After he left, I sampled the champagne and had a blast."

Annie knew she should disapprove, but she was glad that Zoe had found a silver lining of her own. "Maybe after things calm down, you and I can meet quietly, or at least have a phone conversation now and then."

"Sure, that sounds great," Zoe said. "I came down for lunch. Inez should be serving it soon. Maybe you can stay and eat, if Dad doesn't come down. He skipped breakfast."

Annie drew in a breath. "You don't know . . . ." She took Zoe's hand. "Brent fired Inez. Because she brought me my things after I left. He accused her of being disloyal and told her to leave today. I'm taking her to Rancho de la Noche."

Zoe's face paled a bit. "He fired Inez? Oh, God. He's really gone off the deep end. That's the problem, he always thinks he's right, can't see any other point of view. He doesn't understand women and just assumes a successful man like him knows what's best for everyone. He's my dad, and I love him, but he's so exasperating. You were right to escape living here."

"I made the right decision," Annie agreed, "but I didn't foresee it would result in Inez losing her job. And I never thought about my work at the ruin, that Brent would look upon me as a trespasser now. He's punishing me, and I suppose I can't blame him."

"Well, I can," Zoe asserted. "When he calms down, I'll talk to him."

Chapter Six

That evening at dusk, Rafael awoke. When he walked into his living room, he was surprised to see Inez sitting on the couch with Annie. He also noticed clothing and other items piled in a corner.

"Inez," he said with a smile. "Bringing Annie more of her things?"

Inez glanced away and her expression did not look happy. She seemed upset, maybe even a little scared.

Annie stood and walked up to Rafael. "Brent fired her. He found out she helped me and that she knew I was involved with you. She has no place to go, so I brought her here. I didn't think you'd mind."

"Of course not," he said, shocked that Inez had lost the job she'd had for so long. And all because of his relationship with Annie. He turned to Inez. "You are very welcome here."

Inez looked up at him with some relief in her eyes. "Thank you. It would just be until I can figure out where to go. My brother in New Mexico is in poor health. I can't impose on him. I have some cousins I email with a little, but I haven't seen any of them in many years. There's no one who can take me in. I need to look for another job as a cook."

Rafael walked around the low coffee table and sat in the easy chair near the end of the couch where Inez was sitting.

"How about if I hire you?" he said, his mind busy with hope that he had a way to rescue her.

Annie sat down on the couch again, smiling. "That's a wonderful idea."

Inez seemed puzzled. "You don't eat, Rafael."

"But Annie does."

"And I hate to cook. I'd have to live on sandwiches," Annie joked. "I'd miss your beautiful dinners."

"My ranch hands have always fended for themselves," Rafael said. "Never hired anyone to cook for them. Fernando recently mentioned that since his wife died he's been living on frozen food. Which I didn't understand, but couldn't ask him to explain."

Annie laughed. "People can buy frozen meals at the grocery store and then heat them in a microwave. We don't eat them frozen."

Rafael raised his eyebrows, embarrassed at what he didn't know about the modern world. "I can't remember if I've ever been in a grocery store. But now I see what some of the TV commercials are about."

"You watch TV?" Annie pointed to the television in the corner of the living room. "Yours is so old. I tried turning it on, but the reception wasn't very good."

"Only to get the news. I need to buy a new one," he admitted. He looked at Annie. "You should come with me some evening and help me pick one out." He paused with a happy new thought. "And you can be here when they deliver it. I don't have to ask one of the men."

"Sure," Annie agreed. She turned to Inez and her smile disappeared.

Rafael looked at Inez, too, and saw that she still seemed troubled. "What's wrong?"

Inez's eyes met his. "I'm very grateful for your help, Rafael. But I don't know if I'd feel comfortable living here. I mean . . . with our history. And now you're with Annie."

"I see," Rafael said, beginning to understand. She once was his mistress, but now he mainly saw her as an aging woman whose life he had impacted in a profound way. It dawned on him that Inez would still see him as the same man she used to come to when he telepathically called her in the night. He looked the same as he had then, and it brought her back to her past, while his mind stayed in the present.

"Don't worry about that," Annie said. "I understand. I was married and divorced when I was young. Rafael has had many relationships over the centuries. We all come with a past. Inez, you've become sort of a combination sister and mother to me. I'd be so pleased to have you here."

Rafael smiled to himself and glanced downward, too in love with Annie just then to risk letting it show, out of respect for Inez. Annie had a great deal of wisdom for her mere thirty-five years. And he admired her generosity of spirit, her innate kindness.

Tears welled in Inez's brown eyes. "Thank you. But where would I stay? Rafael doesn't exactly have a guest room."

Rafael pondered this. Inez had a good point. "There's an extra room I use for storage. I could have it changed into a bedroom." He straightened as a new thought popped into his mind. "The duplex. I had it built for Francisco, so his daughter and her husband could live there next to him. The husband had lost his job, and he worked here as a ranch hand for several years. But they moved to Tucson, and that half of the duplex is available. It's small, but it's got a kitchen, a living room, bedroom and bathroom."

"That sounds perfect," Annie said, looking at Inez. "Isn't it?"

Inez's eyes were wide with what appeared to be hope marred by worry. "Wouldn't Francisco mind? I'd feel like I was barging in on him."

"I own the house," Rafael said. "It's my decision. Why would he mind?" A thought came to him. "Are you worried about bumping into him? There is a door between the two households, but you can lock it."

Inez nodded but still seemed unsure. "He took me home after I drove Annie's truck here."

"Did he say something you didn't like?" Annie asked.

"One of Brent's men saw him drop me off and decided Francisco and I were having a 'romance.' I think he told Brent, and that's how Brent put it all together."

Annie pensively twisted a lock of her long hair around her finger. "So you're worried that if you're living next to Francisco people will think you're involved with him?"

Inez sighed. "It's not so much what people think. It's what Francisco might think."

Rafael grew baffled as he listened to the two women talk. "Francisco mostly thinks about training our horses."

"Well, he told me I was nice looking and a good cook, and I'd make a great wife. I was . . . speechless."

Annie's eyes widened with excitement. "He likes you."

"Ah, so you're afraid if you move in next to him, he'll take it as a sign that you're interested in him," Rafael said, finally making sense of this female conversation.

Inez lifted her shoulders. "It might even look like I'm chasing after him. I'm not in the market for any romance. Or a husband. I'm happy being alone."

"Happy? Or is it habit?" Annie said. "You once told me that habit replaces happiness."

"It does," Inez replied. "What would I do with a man nosing around me? I'm done with all that."

Rafael couldn't help but wonder if her former relationship with him affected her viewpoint. "I took away your freedom to marry. But now you *are* free. You can be open to the possibility of a romance. I'd like that for you, Inez."

Inez looked at him starkly. "Rafael, when I was nineteen I came to you by horseback one night. My horse got loose and galloped back to the Logan ranch. It was dawn when I discovered the horse was gone. You had retired. I saw Francisco and asked him to drive me home. It was obvious to him that I'd spent the night with his boss. I didn't tell him my name. Seems unlikely, looking at me now, he'd guess I'm the same woman. But what if he does? He'd think less of me. And he might learn your secret. Unless you've told him what you are."

Rafael pulled his mind back several decades. "He was young then. I recall he did say he'd driven a beautiful girl back to the Logan spread and gave me a between-us-guys glint, as immature men do. I used my mental powers to make him forget."

Inez appeared relieved. "Good. Thank you. So he has no idea you're a vampire? Even after working for you so long?"

"I don't think so. But he does seem to accept that there's something different about me. I can't keep making him forget that he only sees me at night. It's not practical. And . . . ," Rafael paused, not wanting to reveal too much concern, "he does avoid making eye contact with me nowadays. Perhaps he's learned that I can control his thoughts when I lock his gaze with mine. Yet, he seems happy here. Training our Appaloosas is his lifelong labor of love. And I feel his respect for me. I believe I've treated him well."

Annie was listening to him attentively, another thing Rafael loved about her. She turned to Inez. "Then there shouldn't be any problem, right? Do you feel better about moving into the duplex?"

Inez nodded in her hesitant way. "I think we should ask Francisco how he feels about it, even if he doesn't own the house."

Rafael smiled and stood. "Let's do that right now."

As the three of them left the house and walked the two minutes it took to get to Francisco's door, Rafael was glad he had the opportunity to do something good for Inez. Once again Inez's life had been changed forever, due to Rafael's choices and actions. All because of his vampire nature. Everyone he touched suffered in some way. How could he protect Annie from harm? He needed to be doubly vigilant and turn away from his former carelessness. Mortals were fragile creatures with only several decades to live their lives. Lives he shouldn't ruin by pursuing his eternal quest for a contented existence. His unquenchable thirst for their blood was also a never-ending burden. He hoped living with Annie would not prove to be too great a temptation for him to resist. If he harmed her, he could never forgive himself.

How he wished he could be an ordinary mortal man again.

# # #

Inez felt self-conscious, even embarrassed, as Rafael knocked on Francisco's door. Francisco greeted them all with a surprised smile.

"Come in," he said and stepped aside so they could enter his living room.

His furnishings were simple. An upholstered chair and couch, a low table, a TV and a bookshelf along one wall. A braided throw rug covered the wood floor. Inez could see his kitchen through the open doorway on the far side of the room. She noticed how neat everything was. No dust. Magazines in a straight pile on the coffee table. No mess anywhere. From what she could see, even the kitchen looked clean and polished.

Francisco nodded to her, brightness in his eyes which seemed to reveal he was pleased to see her in particular. This made Inez nervous. Then Francisco looked at Annie and puzzlement entered his eyes.

"Francisco, I want to introduce you to Annie Carmichael," Rafael said.

Annie and Francisco shook hands.

"She's moved into my house and will be living with me. We're in love and want to be together," Rafael explained.

Francisco took in this news with obvious wonder, and some confusion. "But . . . your name is similar to the woman Brent Logan married. I saw it in the paper."

Annie shook her head. "I didn't marry him as planned. I realized I couldn't because I'd fallen in love with Rafael."

"I whisked her away on horseback," Rafael said. "And Inez, who I understand you've met, drove Annie's truck here with all her belongings. Because of that, Logan fired Inez. I told her she could live here."

Francisco looked crestfallen. "You lost your job as cook?"

Inez bowed her head and nodded.

"So," Rafael continued, "I'm hiring her as our cook. You and the men will be eating well from now on. And I'd like her to live next door to you, in the empty half of the duplex. I hope you won't mind."

"Not at all," Francisco said with enthusiasm. "A wonderful idea. I've always heard good things from Charlie about Inez's cooking. I'd love to have her as my neighbor. This house seems lonely since my daughter and her husband moved out. She kept the place spic and span. They left the furniture. I go in there now and again to make sure no faucets are dripping and so on."

"Okay, then," Rafael said with a grin. "It's settled." He turned to Inez. "Does this all sound okay? We can start getting you moved in right now."

Her head whirling a bit with the quickness of the plans being made, Inez felt relieved. Even hopeful, after the despair she'd felt that morning when Brent fired her.

"I think I'll be happier here than I ever was at the Logans'. I know . . . ," she realized she needed to speak carefully, "I mean, I've heard that you raise Appaloosas. They are so beautiful. It will be a joy to be able to see them when I have some free time."

Rafael placed his hands lightly on her shoulders. "You'll have one of your own. As a welcome gift, you can have your choice of the foals born in the spring. Francisco will train the colt for you as it grows. Won't you?" He glanced at Francisco.

"Of course," Francisco readily agreed, but he looked astonished. "That's quite a gift."

Inez knew the Appaloosas from Rancho de la Noche were worth thousands of dollars. She looked up into Rafael's eyes. "No, I couldn't."

"You love to ride," he said in a very soft voice. "I want you to have a horse of your own."

From the earnestness in Rafael's face, Inez understood that the colt would be more than a welcome gift. He was trying to make up for the past, for taking her blood and keeping her under his power for so long. She felt touched that he seemed to feel guilty now. She had always understood that he couldn't help what he was, his need for blood, for secrecy, and companionship.

She nodded. "Thank you, Rafael. I will treasure your gift."

Inez realized Francisco and Annie were looking on in silence. Annie's smiling eyes had grown misty. Francisco still seemed baffled, yet he questioned nothing and appeared pleased.

"I'll show you the colts when you're ready," Francisco said. "I think there's one in particular that might be just right for you. Pearl Girl." He glanced at Rafael, who quickly nodded, his face beaming in agreement.

"Well, Inez, let's get you moved in," Rafael said, taking Annie's hand as they headed to the door.

Inez couldn't believe her good fortune. A new job. Her own home. An Appaloosa of her own. It was like a dream.

Getting fired was quickly becoming a blessing in disguise.

Chapter Seven

The next evening, after spending the day helping Inez finish getting settled in the duplex and going grocery shopping with her in town, Annie was looking forward to spending some quality time alone with Rafael. They hadn't made love yesterday, and she was looking forward to remedying that.

But just around dusk, when she was anticipating Rafael appearing, her cell phone rang.

"Hey, Annie. It's Zoe. Can I come over? Dad's at a charity dinner. He won't know, and there's no one else to check up on me."

"Sure," Annie replied. "How will you get here?"

"I learned to drive at school. I'll borrow one of the ranch pickups. Is Inez there?"

"She just moved into her own place," Annie said. "You can visit her, too."

"Great! I'll be right there. I know the way."

Annie was closing her cell phone when Rafael came into the living room. They embraced.

"Have you had dinner?" he asked.

"A sandwich. Inez will start cooking tomorrow. I went into town with her to get supplies."

Lights played in Rafael's dark eyes. He slipped his hand under her T-shirt to fondle her breast. "Missed this last night. Too much going on. You'd had a tiring day giving Brent the ring back and helping Inez."

Annie closed her eyes at the pleasure of his touch. She placed her hand over his. "We can't just yet," she told him with aching regret. "Zoe called a minute ago. She's coming over to visit me and see Inez. She'll be here in a little while. Not enough time for us to finish this." She squeezed his hand. "Later. I want you so much."

Rafael acquiesced and reluctantly drew his hand away. "I exist to love you. But I'll wait. Does Brent know his daughter is coming to see you?"

"No. He's not home and she's sneaking away. She's a handful, but she has a good heart. Yesterday she told me she'll try to talk Brent into letting me continue excavating the ruin."

"He said you can't?" Rafael asked with alarm.

"Said he'd regard me, and you, as trespassers."

"What does that mean for your paper? You were going to detail your findings and publish them."

"There's more work I wanted to do at the ruin, but I'll just have to write my paper with what I've got. I'll start teaching again in January. I thought I'd go to the university tomorrow afternoon to see some of my colleagues, catch up on news. Also find my notes for the classes I'll be teaching."

Rafael took her in his arms. "Can you sleep late? I'll be keeping you up a while."

She smiled. "But I'll sleep well."

"Do you have to do a lot of preparation for the classes you teach?" he asked, as if the thought had just come to him.

"Some I've taught for years, so those are easier. But I have some more advanced classes, too. By the way, there's going to be a faculty holiday party the second Saturday in December. It'll be at a professor's home in Tucson. He gives it every year. I have to go. Will you come with me? It's a long drive just for a party, but we can leave at sunset and arrive before it's over."

Rafael's expression grew troubled and he appeared doubtful. He was about to reply when they were interrupted by the sound of a vehicle pulling up on the gravel driveway outside. Soon there was a knock at the door.

"Maybe I should answer it," Annie said. "Zoe hasn't met you."

Rafael nodded and let her go.

Annie opened the front door. "Zoe," she said, smiling at seeing the teen's young face. "You look so cute. Come in."

The girl was dressed in leggings, a tunic top, and the jacket Brent had bought her for her Halloween costume. She'd dressed up as Katniss from *The Hunger Games*. As she walked into the room, she saw Rafael and stopped in her tracks.

"Zoe, I'd like you to meet Rafael de la Vega," Annie said.

"A pleasure," Rafael said with a polite smile.

"OMG," Zoe said under her breath as she stared at him. "You're Rafael? Really? I never thought . . ." She turned to Annie, wide-eyed. "I can see why you picked him over Dad. He's gorgeous!" she said in a pretend whisper loud enough to carry through the room. She turned back to gape at Rafael again. "Do you have any younger brothers?"

Rafael silently laughed. "No, I don't. But thank you for the compliment."

"I could come up with a pocketful more," Zoe said. "I mean, you are seriously handsome."

Annie choked a bit with giggles. "Would you like to sit down?"

"Sure," Zoe said, and plopped down on the leather easy chair as Rafael and Annie sat together on the sofa.

"When will your dad be home?" Annie asked, composing herself. "He'll be mad if he finds out you're here."

"Yeah, but I can handle him. He told me he'll be home about nine. I've got time," Zoe said blithely. "So, guess what? I think I convinced him to let you keep on working at the ruin."

"No. How?" Annie asked, afraid to hope.

"I confronted him," Zoe answered. "Here's exactly what I said." She proceeded to quote herself with pride. "'Just because Annie didn't want to be controlled by you isn't a reason to banish her from the ruin. Archeology is her life. And that ruin was here long before you were born or any Logan owned the property. How can you say it's yours? It's part of our national heritage. You never gave it a thought before Annie came.'"

Annie grinned. "Bravo! You really gave that speech some thought."

"Remarkable," Rafael agreed, looking impressed. "From one so young. Thank you for standing up for Annie."

"What did Brent say?" Annie asked, holding her breath.

"Nothing for about a minute. He sort of paced around his office. And then he mumbled, 'Okay, I'll let Annie excavate the ruin.'" Zoe glanced at Rafael. "But he said if you ever set foot there, he'd look upon you as a trespasser. Sorry. I figured I'd better not argue, or he might get mad again and change his mind about Annie."

Rafael nodded. "You know your father. That was wise. I'm glad Annie can finish her work."

Annie felt a wave of relief. "Thank you, Zoe. I'll never be your stepmom, and I feel some regret about that. But I never had a sister. Can we pretend I've adopted you as my younger sister?"

Zoe's blue eyes grew big. "Cool! I'm an only child, so I'd love to have you as my big sister." She got up and hugged Annie around the shoulders. Annie gave her a kiss on the cheek.

"How's school?" Annie asked as Zoe sat down again.

The teenager rolled her eyes. "I'm supposed to read *Pride and Prejudice* and write a paper on it."

"Jane Austen is my favorite author," Annie said. "Call if you need some help."

"Why couldn't we study *The Hunger Games*?" Zoe lamented.

Annie chuckled. "You look great in that jacket, by the way. I remember when you got it for your Katniss costume."

"And just like you said, I could wear it as an everyday jacket after Halloween. I got lots of compliments on my costume. Carrying Dad's old bow and arrow made it perfect. That's all thanks to you. Dad was ready to ground me because I wanted to go as Cat Woman in that slinky outfit. Your idea saved the day."

"I remember," Annie said with a sigh. "When I went shopping with you and Brent that day, I thought maybe I could fit into your family. It was a good day. But in the end, I had to choose Rafael." She turned her gaze to Rafael sitting beside her. "My soul mate."

"Well, duh," Zoe exclaimed. "I don't think Dad could be anybody's soul mate."

"I hope in time he'll be happy," Annie said.

"Me, too," Zoe agreed. "He's not exactly fun to live with at the moment. And the house is so empty without Inez."

"Has he hired a new cook?" Annie asked.

"He started interviewing a few applicants. Meanwhile he's had a caterer in town bring meals over and grumbles about the expense. I think he regrets firing Inez, but he'd never admit it."

"She's settled in nicely here. I'll take you to see her, if you like," Annie said.

"That would be great," Zoe replied.

Annie rose to leave and Zoe followed suit. The girl smiled at Rafael with admiring eyes once more, said goodbye and left with Annie.

Annie brought her to the duplex and knocked on Inez's door.

"She's got her own house?" Zoe said, amazed. "Wow, she must be thrilled."

When Inez answered and saw Zoe, the two immediately hugged. Inez invited them in. Annie stayed and chatted for a few minutes, then left Zoe to have a heart to heart talk with Inez. She walked back to the ranch house, where Rafael was waiting for her.

"They have a lot to chat about, so I came back," Annie said, walking up to him as he rose to greet her. She slipped her arms around his neck. "So, Mr. Gorgeous, how about showing me what you've got in store for me."

Rafael broke into a smile. "Zoe says what she thinks. It's been a long time since I've been around a teenage girl. I didn't expect all that admiration."

"She's maturing though. What she said to Brent showed a good amount of logic and wisdom. I'm proud of her."

Rafael's face grew somber. "I can see how you and she have formed a fond attachment. It's my fault that she's without a stepmother who would have been very good for her. One more life I've impacted in a negative way."

Annie felt confused and a little disturbed by his misgivings. "It couldn't be helped, Rafael. It's no one's fault."

He smiled at her tenderly. "You are so sweet. I don't know what I would have done if you hadn't chosen me." He leaned in to kiss her.

Anxious to lie with him, she eagerly returned his kiss with passion. He picked her up in his arms and carried her to bed.

Hours later, naked, her long hair disheveled, she fell asleep in Rafael's arms, limp with voluptuous exhaustion, totally and exquisitely fulfilled.

# # #

Around four a.m., while Annie was sleeping soundly, Rafael began to feel the hunger for blood. Hours of intensely satisfying sex had depleted some of his energy. He gazed at his beloved. Annie's beautiful hair was spread over the pillow, exposing her delicate throat. The soft pulse of her carotid caught his eye. Immediately, a powerful yearning to taste her blood rose inside him. The unholy urge threatened to overtake him.

Absolutely no! Gently, but quickly, he slipped out of her embrace without waking her. He got off the bed, chastising himself for even thinking of falling into the temptation of drinking from her. There were blood bags in his refrigerator. He could feed without harming anyone.

And yet, as he walked out of the room, the wild, savage aspect of his vampire nature welled up inside him. He hated it when that feeling came upon him. From his first moments awaking as a vampire in 1540, the ferocious need for blood had overcome him. A gypsy curse had fulfilled itself on his thirtieth birthday, when he'd been attacked by an evil manifestation in the form of a wolf. He'd clawed his way out of the desert earth, where his fellow conquistadors had buried his dead body, never thinking he would rise again. A good thing they'd moved on, or he would have attacked one of them, blind to anything but his terrible hunger.

Over the following years, he'd learned to control himself, learned that he could feed from animals, though he drew his greatest strength from human blood. He'd sought out attractive women, drunk from them and put them under his power, in part to appease his sexual desire but also to have a ready and willing source from which to fulfill his need for blood. Inez had been his last such victim-mistress, the one he'd had for the longest time, three decades. To see and understand now how he'd altered her life in such a negative way convicted him more than anything else of the shame and guilt he ought to feel. He needed to subdue his urge to feed completely when he was near Annie, the beautiful gift he didn't merit or deserve. He must never take her blood. How could he forgive himself if he did?

But that savage restlessness was upon him again. Fortunately, he'd learned the best way to assuage his need. Still naked from loving Annie, he walked outside, concentrated, and shape-shifted into his wolf self.

Rafael bounded away from the ranch house, in a different direction from the stables and corral, out over the desert. Through the scrubby chaparral that blanketed the land, lit only by moonlight, he headed to Logan's property, moving swiftly on all fours, even faster than a natural wolf could run. The cool air breezing over his snout and past his ears began to fulfill his craving for wild freedom, something he had to keep severely under control in human form. He moved as fast and as quietly as the night wind.

The duality of his existence had become increasingly clear as decades and centuries had gone by, but since meeting Annie, his double nature had begun to tear at his soul. If indeed he still had a soul. Annie knew he could shape-shift. When he'd first approached her, in wolf form, after he'd discovered her working at the Anasazi ruin, his cherished resting place, he'd tried to scare her away. He'd pretended to be ready to pounce on her, and she'd shot him. She'd wept over him and tried to comfort him when she thought he was dying. But he recovered, of course, and after that he couldn't help but admire and love her. She once even called him a puppy-dog.

She didn't understand how brutal he could be. Like now. As Rafael came upon a steer in Logan's pasture, separated from the rest of the herd, he didn't hesitate. He jumped at the animal, brought it to the ground, tore open its neck and feasted on the warm blood that poured from the wounded artery. Rafael's vampire nature allowed him to do this almost silently. The rest of the dozing herd was not disturbed. He fed quickly, felt satiated and empowered with renewed strength. Brimming with energy, enjoying his ecstatic freedom to roam and run as he pleased, he bounded off and covered more ground, traveling maybe twenty miles until even he had had enough. He slowed his pace as he came back onto his own land and approached his house.

As he passed by the duplex, he saw Inez standing on the small porch of her new home, pulling her long robe close around her. A lamp fixture near her door provided a dim circle of light behind her. His fur was black, hard to see in the dark, but Inez apparently noticed some movement and she jumped backward. He slowed his trot and walked up to her.

"Rafael?" She peered at him as he sat on his haunches about three feet away.

In wolf form he could not speak. He could howl, but that would wake up everyone. Instead, he opened his mouth like an ordinary dog and panted in a happy way.

Inez smiled. "You needed to run."

He nodded, then cocked his head and looked at her in a questioning way.

"I woke up early. Couldn't get back to sleep. So I came outside to see the sunrise from my new home." Her expression changed. "You'll need to get back to your coffin soon," she said with concern. Then, apparently remembering, she added, "But your wolf fur protects you a little, doesn't it. Still, it's time." She looked past him. "I can see the first light on the horizon."

He hung his head.

"Rafael, you have Annie now. Living with you. You'll be happy with her." Inez said this in a reassuring voice. She knew him better than he would have wished anyone to. Stepping forward and reaching out, she touched his ear and ran her hand under his chin.

But then with alarm, she drew her hand back and looked at it. "Blood. You've fed."

He couldn't help but notice the revulsion in her eyes that she was trying to hide. He rose on all fours, looked at her, then trotted away, stopping near the water trough inside the corral. Jumping the fence, he dipped his head into the water to wash away the blood. After bounding back over the fence, he walked to the kitchen door at the back of the house, shape-shifted into human form and entered.

After peeking in on Annie, who was still serenely asleep, he went to his coffin down the hidden staircase from the kitchen pantry. He wondered how long he could keep up this dual existence. Even Inez, who understood him best, could still be repulsed at the steer's blood left on him from his night kill. Would Annie be able to fully accept the whole of his vampire nature? Would his savage impulses get the worst of him someday? Could he keep Annie safe from himself?

These questions weighing on his mind, Rafael closed the lid of his coffin just as he could feel the early rays of morning light outside weakening him into a lethargic stupor.

# # #

Later that morning, Inez began cooking breakfast in the small kitchen in her duplex. The modern stove and sink were in much better shape than their counterparts in Rafael's house. Not sure when Annie or the men would be ready to eat, she decided to make quiche, which could be eaten warm or after it had cooled, and a salad of mixed fruits. She brought a serving of both and left it in Rafael's kitchen for Annie, who apparently had not awakened yet. Then, noticing a child's wagon outside Francisco's door— she wondered if he'd bought it for visiting grandchildren—she borrowed it to bring breakfast to the small bunkhouse next to the large stables. Knocking on the door, she was greeted with the happy faces of the several men who lived there. They helped her set it on the table inside, from which they cleared away the pack of playing cards and set of dominoes. They'd made their own coffee already, which Inez had anticipated, as this was what the Logan ranch hands did as well.

Since Francisco lived in the duplex, she realized she had to serve him separately. So she knocked on his door. He answered and greeted her with eager eyes, which shone even more enthusiastically when he saw the quiche and fruit she'd brought.

"Come in and eat with me," he said.

Taken by surprise, Inez quickly replied, "I've already eaten. Thank you."

"Oh. Well, I thought I'd help you choose the colt Rafael wishes to give you. Maybe in about a half hour? Knock on the inside door between your place and mine, and I'll take you to the corral."

"Okay, but I . . . I'll knock on your front door." She told him this forthrightly and then stepped off of his small front porch to walk back to her own porch. She entered her house and her eyes went to the door that connected her living room with his. Though she could keep the deadbolt twisted shut from her side, and she did, it still bothered her that this connection to Francisco's place existed. She wondered if he kept the deadbolt locked on his door, just on the other side of hers.

A half hour later, she knocked on his front door. In only a moment, he opened it and greeted her with a smile, carrying a small, transparent plastic bag of cut up carrots in his hand.

"This way," he told her and walked alongside her with a jaunty step. "We have a beautiful colt with a sweet disposition that Rafael and I think you'll like. Her daddy is Old Business, one of our grand champions." He pointed. "There she is there, near her mother, My Blue Heaven."

He opened the wooden corral gate and they walked into the large enclosure.

"Do you worry about the black wolf in these parts?" Inez posed the question in an innocent tone, wondering how Francisco would respond. "Brent Logan tried to shoot the wolf several times, but his aim must have been bad."

"I've seen the wolf at night now and then. Seems almost tame. Never bothers our horses. An Indian man from one of the local reservations told me that they believe the wolf is a protective spirit."

"I've heard that," Inez told him truthfully.

"This man said that one of their young children, a three-year old boy, wandered off from his home. His mother was frantic when night fell and no one had found the child. And then out of the dark, the black wolf appeared with the lost child riding on his back. The wolf brought the kid home unharmed. After the boy ran to his mother, everyone stared at the animal in astonishment. The Indian said they perceived something mystical about him, especially his eyes. The wolf stared back, then turned and ran off into the dark."

Inez smiled. "I hadn't heard that particular story. When did it happen?"

"Oh, a dozen years ago or so. That wolf must be getting old. Shame that Logan wants to shoot it."

"I know," she said with a sigh. "I tried to tell him the local Indians revere the creature. There have been other such stories over the decades. But . . . the wolf does kill Brent's cattle."

"A wolf's got to eat, I suppose," Francisco said affably as they approached a foal about six months old standing near a graceful mare. The colt's mother had a reddish-brown coat with a blond mane and tail. She had a prominent blanket of speckled white over her rump, a classic Appaloosa characteristic.

"Rafael named this colt Pearl Girl," Francisco said, patting the colt's neck. "He said the white spots that form her blanket look like pearls on sand. Her coat is a lighter brown than her mother's, but it may darken as she grows up. Her mane and tail may stay blond."

Inez looked at the beautiful foal, realizing tears were welling in her eyes. She reached out to touch the white patch on Pearl Girl's nose. "What a sweetheart." Inez smiled as the colt lifted its nose to meet her hand. "Her eyes are so big."

"I think she likes you," Francisco said, as Pearl Girl stepped closer to Inez, seeming eager to make friends. "But Rafael did tell me you're welcome to look at the other colts and choose which you like best."

Inez stroked the colt's warm neck. "Oh, no. I'm already smitten." She turned to Francisco. "She really is mine?"

"Rafael wants you to have her. I've never seen him give anyone a prize colt before. You must be special. How do you know him?"

Inez grew silent, exhaling as she wondered how to answer. "Long story. I met him years ago. He told me then that he raises Appaloosas because they were first brought over by the Spanish conquistadors. And of course, later they were captured and bred by the Nez Perce. Rafael knows history. When he found out I'm half Pueblo Indian, he told me how badly he thought the Spanish treated my people. He's Spanish, perhaps you know."

Francisco nodded. "He did mention that years ago."

"And so . . . I think maybe this is his way of trying to make up for what his ancestors did to my ancestors." She pondered what she was saying, hoping it sounded plausible, for there was indeed some truth to it. "And, well, maybe he feels bad for me that Brent fired me. He's given me a job here. And Pearl Girl to cheer me up." She hugged the colt. "Which she certainly has."

Francisco studied Inez with a keen, yet kindly gaze. "You look so happy. Your eyes always have a natural luster, but they are beaming now. They reveal your warm, beautiful soul."

Inez glanced away, astonished, unsure how to react. "Thank you." No one had ever said such things to her. She grew quiet, petted Pearl Girl, and couldn't think of another thing to say.

"I'll leave you two to get acquainted. She'll eat these out of your hand," Francisco said, handing her the bag of carrots.

As he walked away, Inez pondered his reputation for understanding horses. Apparently he understood people, too. Maybe a little more than she liked.

Or, maybe she could grow accustomed to such attention. Could she? Surely it would take some getting used to!

Chapter Eight

Later that morning, Annie drove to Tucson and stopped first at her condo to see that everything was okay. Her neighbor had been kind enough to look in on her home every few days while Annie was spending her semester sabbatical working at the Anasazi ruin and living at the Logan ranch. But her sabbatical was drawing to a close.

Time to think about the classes she'd be teaching in the spring semester. She left her place and drove to the nearby University of Arizona campus with its stately, red brick buildings, palm trees and green areas. She entered the building where her small office was located, along the same hall with other archeology professors' offices. After hunting through her files for outlines of lectures for her upcoming spring classes, which would include *Pueblo Archeology* and *Archeology of the Southwest*, she found they were all in order. She tucked them away again for now, since classes wouldn't start until mid-January, and it was only Thanksgiving week.

Annie walked down the hall to the faculty coffee room, a small functional room with a K-cup machine, a tiny sink, shelves with professors' personal cups, and a couple of square tables with four chairs each. She was happy to find two of her colleagues there, Joan Wilcox and Tom Harvey. Both had been promoted to full professor in the last few years.

"Well, look what the cat dragged in," Tom said jovially when he saw her walk in.

Joan's blond head turned and she smiled when she saw Annie. "Hey! Haven't seen you in a while. Come on, sit down."

Tom, always polite, rose and pulled out a chair for Annie. He was a bit overweight, pushing forty, had a freckled face and a full head of red hair. Annie knew how careful he needed to be when working on digs to wear a big hat. He'd experienced his share of bad sunburns.

"Can I get you some coffee?" he asked.

"Okay, thanks," Annie said.

As he set about putting a K-cup in the machine, Joan asked, "How are things going at the Logan ruin?" She had a broad, sunny face, with vivid blue eyes and a trim figure under her khaki pants and pullover sweater.

"Pretty good. Not as far along as I'd like. I got a little sidetracked," Annie admitted.

"Sidetracked?" Joan asked.

"Almost got married."

"What?" Joan said.

Obviously startled, Tom turned with the full coffee cup in his hand and it almost spilled. "Married? To whom?" he asked as he set the steaming cup in front of her.

"Brent Logan," Annie said quietly. "But it didn't work out. He's not too happy with me, but I hear he's going to let me continue work at the ruin."

"Good thing," Joan said. "That ruin is a plus for you, since you'll be providing a new dig site for students taking the hands-on excavation classes."

"Yes, I hope so," Annie said. "You know, after six years of tenure as associate professor, I can ask to be promoted to full professor. I realize I'm a little young, but I have a few feathers in my cap."

"I'll say," Tom agreed, taking his seat again at the table. "All those articles you've published. More than me. Helps being single, I think. No spouse and kids."

"You may be right," Annie said, "but I'm a little envious of your happy family." She turned to Joan. "You, too."

"Well, my kids are in college now. At forty-three, I'm finally having a little more time to write. So, you're still single?"

Annie cleared her throat. "Not exactly. There's a new man in my life." She began to be careful about what she said.

"Really." Joan sounded impressed. "That's fast work. Almost married, now on to someone new."

"The last few months have been quite an experience," Annie said. "I didn't marry Brent because I fell for   for someone unique and wonderful."

"Bring him to the holiday party," Tom said, "so we can meet him. Gary's having it the second weekend in December, as always." Dr. Gary Hogan was the eldest, and most beloved, archeology professor at the University. He enjoyed throwing the annual party at his home.

"I mentioned it to him." Annie remembered the doubtful look on Rafael's face. "But he didn't seem too keen on coming."

"Well, you better be there," Joan said. She glanced at Tom. "Should we tell her the scuttlebutt?"

Tom nodded and Joan glanced at the open door. She got up to close it, then sat down again. Keeping her voice low, she said, "Annie, news has leaked that you are being considered for the Outstanding Contribution to the Field of Archeology Award."

Annie drew in a breath of excitement. "Honestly? You're sure?" She'd been hoping she might be considered for the prestigious award. If she won it, it would make it more likely that she would get promoted to full professor.

"But," Joan continued, "Frank Florescu is also being considered for the award. He's been openly lobbying for it for months. The five professors on the award selection committee are supposed to remain anonymous. But as usual, it's the worst kept secret among the faculty."

Annie nodded. "I've been away. Who are they this year?"

Tom kept his voice low and named the five professors. "We've seen Frank shamelessly cozying up to them. So you'd better show up at the holiday party and put yourself in front of them. Because it's for sure Frank will be there schmoozing them."

Leaning back in her chair, Annie felt a little disheartened. Frank Florescu was an associate professor, like Annie, but older, in his mid-forties. Though born in the United States, of Romanian parents, he seemed to have acquired old world ideas about women. Last year he'd even chosen to say, right in front of Annie, that he didn't think women should be promoted beyond associate professor. Annie sensed that he seemed to find her in particular, with all her accomplishments, irritating. If she, a female and younger than he, should win the award and even be promoted ahead of him, she knew he would take it as a major insult.

"Don't worry. I'll be at the party," Annie said. "It's one of those optional-yet-mandatory events anyway. Dr. Hogan is a lovely man, but we all know how stiff and formal faculty parties can be."

"Yup," Tom agreed. "Your boyfriend better wear a jacket and tie."

Annie blinked. Did Rafael even own a modern coat and tie?

"And there's a new fly in the ointment you should know," Joan said. "Rumor has it that the powers-that-be in charge of promotions have decided it's been too easy to make full professor in recent years. So next semester they will promote only one person. Most likely, it'll be you and Frank vying for full professorship."

"Fingers crossed you win the award," Tom added. "That will give you the advantage."

"Yikes," Annie muttered. Behind-the-scenes faculty politics could be ruthless.

Joan patted Annie's hand reassuringly. "I suspect most people would root for you. Florescu is such a narcissistic creep. You know, he was a couple of years ahead of me in grad school. He seemed to have so much potential then. Wrote a brilliant dissertation and was a star student. Everyone expected that he'd become prominent in the field, make some big archeological breakthrough. But it hasn't happened. He seems to have peaked too early. Sometimes I almost feel sorry for him. He must be disappointed with how his career is turning out." Joan beamed at her. "Instead, it looks like you're the one who will make her mark, Annie."

Annie left Tucson that evening, after stopping in town to shop, feeling increasingly positive about the chances that her career might be about to take a leap forward early next year. Only about a month and a half to wait. As she headed her truck north toward Rancho de la Noche, she grew eager to tell Rafael about her future prospects.

# # #

After he'd risen at sundown, Rafael walked through his house, but didn't see Annie. He knew she'd driven to Tucson. Perhaps she was on her way home. He schooled himself not to worry.

He left the house, walked to Inez's and knocked on her door. She invited him in.

"Francisco introduced you to Pearl Girl?"

"She's just beautiful, Rafael," Inez gushed, her hands clasped over her heart. "I love her already. Are you sure you want to give her away? Francisco said her sire is a grand champion."

"She's yours," Rafael said, exuberant that he'd made her happy.

"I told Francisco that I knew you felt bad that the Spanish were so cruel to the Pueblo Indians, and that you probably gave me the colt to make amends. And because Brent fired me." Inez was wringing her hands now. "I hope that sounded okay. He seemed to be wondering."

Rafael nodded. "I *am* glad I can finally do something for you. To make amends. Francisco doesn't need to know exactly what for." After asking her if she was comfortable in her half of the duplex, he wished her goodnight.

He walked to Francisco's door and knocked. Francisco invited him in.

"Inez is happier than I've ever seen her. Thank you for bringing her to meet Pearl Girl."

Francisco shrugged. "Sure. It was a beautiful moment. Inez's eyes teared up and she was really touched. It's too bad you missed her reaction. Wish you'd presented her the colt yourself."

Rafael stiffened a bit. He tried to catch Francisco's gaze, but as always nowadays, Francisco avoided eye contact. He couldn't make the horse trainer forget, so he fell back on a story he'd improvised years ago.

"I wish I could have, too. But sunlight just hurts my eyes too much. It's my extreme sensitivity to the sun, so I stay indoors. Even sunglasses don't help." He'd been telling this falsehood for so long, he wondered if Francisco was beginning to believe it. He tried to read his mind, but Francisco managed to continue evading eye contact. It made Rafael nervous. Just how much did Francisco know, or intuit?

Francisco smiled, glancing at the inside door to Inez's half of the duplex. "Well, your loss is my gain. I got to know Inez better. She's usually a closed person, but today I got a glimpse of the warm heart she hides."

"Good," Rafael said, surprised and pleased. Had Francisco taken a shine to Inez? Wouldn't that be something. He'd be happy to see Francisco become the new man in Inez's life. The upstanding, mortal man that she'd never had. "Good," he repeated. "You'll let her watch when you train Pearl Girl?"

"That's my plan," Francisco said with enthusiasm. For a fleeting fraction of a second, he met Rafael's gaze. Long enough for Rafael to read Francisco's heart and mind, so full of hope and optimism.

They discussed how the various horses were coming along in their training, which ones were ready for sale to the right owner. Both Rafael and Francisco were particular about being sure that each of their Appaloosas went to people who would love and properly care for them. Rafael's foreman, who managed the ranch, tended to be more concerned about making money, so between them they were constantly educating the foreman as to what his priorities should be. When it came to horses and the ranch, Rafael and Francisco had been on the same wavelength for decades, which allowed Rafael to put full trust in him while Rafael rested in his coffin during daylight hours. It was why he worried what would happen to their friendship if Francisco ever found out the truth about his boss.

Rafael bid him goodnight and stepped outside just as Annie drove up in her white pickup. He strode over to greet her. She threw her arms around him and bubbled with excitement.

"I'm up for an award and maybe a promotion to full professor," she said as they walked inside. She went on to fill him in on all the details, explaining parts he didn't understand. He'd attended the

98

university in Salamanca, Spain before he became a
conquistador bound for the New World. But that was
hundreds of years ago, and university life sounded
quite different now, from what Annie described.

She carried what looked like a bag of clothing
over her arm. A clothes hanger hung out from one
end.

"You bought yourself something new?" he asked.

"For you," she said, unzipping the bag. "For the
holiday party I mentioned. You'll need to be dressed
up. Faculty parties tend to be a little formal." She
pulled out the hanger and held up a brown jacket and
a striped tie. "I took one of your shirts along and the
salesman helped me estimate your size. If it's wrong,
I can return it."

Rafael stepped back. "I've never worn one of
those neckties. Don't even know how to tie the knot."

"I do," she said. "My father never could do it
neatly enough, so I learned and tied it for him. It's a
windsor knot. A little tricky, but we'll manage. Good
thing you have some white shirts. Where do you buy
them?"

"Catalogs." He felt uneasy, took the clothes from
her and set them on the leather couch, not anxious to
try them on. "I'll be out of place at your party. On
those rare occasions when I've been in a roomful of
mortals, I never feel at ease. Afraid they'll sense I'm
different."

"When I first met you, I didn't sense it," she told him in a reassuring tone. "You had to tell me, even explain to me that vampires really exist. You'll be a bit different in your look and manner. You're a little old world. You speak with an accent. And you'll be the sexiest guy in the room. But other than that--"

"My teeth? I can't see my face in a mirror, but the incisors feel sharp."

She subtly nodded. "They are pointy. But I've seen mortal men and women who have pointed incisors, too. Yours may be a little sharper, but people would have to look close to see that. As Zoe said, you're 'seriously handsome.' Who's going to notice your teeth? Not the women. They'll be admiring your other attributes. And the men will be envious of your looks and bearing."

He took her in his arms. "You're painting quite a picture."

"You *will* be quite a picture at the party. Not the usual professor or spouse. We're a boring lot. You'll be exotic and fascinating. People may stare at you, but not in a bad way."

"Sounds like an ordeal. Must I go?" He didn't like to disappoint her, but if there was any way out of this situation, he aimed to find it.

Annie slipped her arms around his neck, her mouth in an adorable pout. "I have to go. People who decide who gets the award and who gets promoted will be there. I already told a couple of my colleagues that I have a new boyfriend. Everyone brings their spouse or significant other. We *are* living together. I want you to be part of my life, my entire life. I've been on sabbatical and I need to go back to campus life. Attending dull faculty parties is part of that. With you there, it won't be dull."

Rafael listened, taking in the fact that out of love and respect for Annie, he needed to play the role of *boyfriend*, a modern term he found silly. He was far from boyhood. But he wanted her to continue her life in as usual a way as possible. If accompanying her to this party was what she needed him to do, then he would do his best to be a boyfriend.

"All right," he said with an exhale. "Do I have to wear the tie?"

She pondered a moment. "Oh, I guess not. I want you to be comfortable. When we tell people you raise Appaloosas, lack of a tie will make sense."

"Thank God. Not that the Almighty pays attention to me anymore." He gave her a squeeze. "Inez left you a dinner to warm up. And after you've eaten, I'd love to make love. If you're not too tired."

She grinned. "Never too tired for that."

Chapter Nine

Annie spent the next weeks working at the Anasazi ruin and writing her paper about her excavation. The *Journal of Archeology* would be publishing it. If Brent knew she spent time at the ruin, he left her alone. And Brent had no idea that some days Rafael rested in the kiva while she worked. When the sun set they made love, just as they had at the beginning of their relationship. The ancient broken walls of the Anasazi ruin had brought them together, and now provided them a serene, romantic, spiritual place that was theirs alone to share. Annie thought her life could not be more perfect. Rafael seemed happy and at peace, too.

On the second Saturday of December, the day of the party, she and Rafael drove to Tucson shortly after sunset. When they reached Dr. Hogan's big home in an upscale neighborhood several miles from the university campus, she parked her pickup and turned to Rafael. In the light coming through the windshield from a nearby streetlamp, she could see that he looked apprehensive, but very handsome in his brown blazer, white shirt and no tie. With his wavy black hair combed back, and not so unruly as usual, he looked like a tamer version of himself. Though Annie preferred him untamed, she was happy that he'd made the effort to conform to polite society for the evening.

His deep brown eyes settled on her. "What's our host's name again?"

"Dr. Gary Hogan. He's our most experienced professor. White hair and glasses. Very kindly man. His wife is lovely, too." She paused. "There will be some students milling around with trays of hors d'oeuvres and wine. And there will be a buffet table with finger food."

His brows quirked in a puckish expression. "People eat fingers?"

She laughed. "Small sandwiches, cut up veggies, little quiches. Things you can pick up with your fingers and eat. No need for a knife and fork."

"I'll just stay away," he muttered.

"If anyone encourages you to eat something, say you've already eaten," Annie suggested.

He nodded grimly. "I did drink down one of my blood bags while you were changing. Figured I'd need extra strength to get through this."

She reached for his hand and squeezed it. "I do appreciate you doing this for me."

His eyes shone as he gazed at her. "For you, anything. Besides, you look stunning in those clothes. I've never seen you dressed so elegantly."

"Thank you." She almost told him it was the cream-colored silk suit she'd bought to wear as her wedding dress. But she decided Rafael didn't need to know that.

Thank goodness she hadn't gotten a full-fledged wedding gown, which was what Brent had wanted her to buy. At first she doubted she'd ever wear the knee length skirt and matching jacket, but when the holiday party came up, she realized it would do perfectly.

"Never saw you with your hair pinned up on top of your head either," he said. "You look beautiful, but I'm aching to pull it down and muss you up."

Annie raised her eyebrow in an impishly seductive way. "Later. When we get home."

His eyes warmed at her provocative promise. "How long do we have to stay?"

"Oh, at least a couple of hours."

"Well, let's go in and start getting it over with," he said.

They walked up to the stately brick house and knocked. A student helper let them in. They entered a spacious living room with Aubusson carpets, antique furniture, and oil paintings on the walls. The place was already brimming with people. The university had a sizeable archeology faculty. Everyone looked well-dressed and on extra polite behavior.

As Annie wound her way through the guests, followed by Rafael, she noticed with secret pleasure that her colleagues, male and female, were giving the man behind her second and third curious, even awed, glances. As if people were wondering, *Who is he? That's the man in Annie's life? She's doing okay!*

She introduced Rafael to their host and hostess, mentioning that he raised Appaloosas. A small group gathered round as Dr. Hogan and his wife took an interest and began asking questions. Mrs. Hogan, it turned out, had been thinking of buying a horse for their granddaughter's birthday.

Rafael, putting on his most gracious manner, answered their questions, his passion for Appaloosas apparent.

As he was involved in conversation, Joan, dressed in red, came up to Annie and pulled her aside. "This is your new guy?" she whispered, her blue eyes bright. "Honey, the women here are all abuzz. He's so handsome. And you're glowing. It's obvious you're having a fabulous extracurricular life!"

"Obvious?" Annie whispered back with astonishment. "It's true, but I didn't think it showed." She started laughing.

"Oh, it shows," Joan said, laughing, too. "Just the way you look at him. And he seems totally devoted. Those brooding brown eyes of his dote on you."

Annie nodded. "He is devoted to me. It's almost like he worships me. I've never had a man treat me that way before, like I was so special. We're very much in love."

Joan sighed in a romantic way. "I'm so happy for you." She gave Annie a quick hug. But then her eyes seemed to focus on someone behind Annie. "There he is, Frank Florescu just coming in. Alone. Always seems to have trouble finding a date."

Annie turned to look. Florescu, who was tall, very slim, with thinning brown hair, immediately caught her gaze. He nodded to her in a curt way. Annie nodded back, instinctively understanding by his body language that he knew she was his competition for the award and full professorship, and he wasn't one to make any pretense of camaraderie. She wondered if his brusque demeanor was his way of covering up an underlying insecurity.

Facing Joan again, Annie said, "Wish I hadn't turned around."

"It's a big party. Won't be hard to avoid him," Joan said. "Don't forget to schmooze with the not so anonymous award committee members. In fact, introduce them to your Rafael, especially the women."

Annie chuckled, but decided to take Joan's advice. She stepped back to stand beside Rafael again. His lively discussion with Mrs. Hogan about an Appaloosa for the Hogans' granddaughter seemed to be nearing an end. As she waited, Annie noticed a young blond fellow in a U of A sweater snapping photos with a cell phone.

Dr. Hogan stepped away from his wife's side for a moment to say to Annie, "That's my grandson, Alan. He's a freshman. I asked him to take some pictures at the party to post on the bulletin board in the faculty room."

Annie smiled. "Nice idea. He's a dapper-looking young man."

When Rafael's conversation with a pleased Mrs. Hogan had finished, Annie took his hand and brought him over to where a couple of the award committee professors, two middle-aged ladies, were standing, holding plates of food. She introduced Rafael, who greeted them in his most courtly, old world manner, which seemed to immediately enchant them. But then Annie glanced at Frank Florescu, who was approaching. It looked fairly obvious that he intended to horn in on them.

Before Florescu reached them, however, young Alan hurried up and began snapping photos of their group of four. "Smile," he eagerly said. Quickly he checked the pictures he'd taken as they appeared in the small screen of his cell phone. With a surprised grin, he looked at Rafael. "Hey, you aren't showing up in my photos. That's weird." He laughed as if it were all a joke. "Are you a ghost or something?"

Annie twined her arm around Rafael's, and she felt his muscles tense.

"I don't like to be photographed," Rafael told Alan in a quiet but absolute manner.

"Okay," Alan said. "Sorry." He moved on to a nearby cluster of guests.

Totally perplexed, Annie whispered to Rafael, "What's wrong?"

"Can't explain here. Later," he told her, his eyes full of alarm.

Just then, Florescu walked up to them. He gave the two older professors a quick nod, then turned to Annie. "Dr. Carmichael," he greeted her tersely. "Introduce me to your friend."

Annoyed at his authoritarian manner, Annie nevertheless did as he asked. "Dr. Florescu, this is Rafael de la Vega."

Rafael still seemed distracted with Alan's joking, but he turned to Florescu and smiled a bit, extending his hand.

Florescu did not shake hands. Instead, Annie saw his eyes focus on Rafael's mouth. The arrogant professor suddenly turned absolutely pale. He stepped backward, looking like he might faint. Rafael reached to steady him, but as their eyes met for an instant, Florescu panicked, turned away and hurried off. Rafael watched him go, looking shaken and grim himself.

"Is Frank sick or something?" one of the women professors asked the other, astonished.

"What's going on?" Annie asked, taking Rafael's elbow and making him step away from the two ladies.

"We have to leave," Rafael told her.

"Why?"

"He knows. I read his mind for an instant when he looked me in the eye." He paused. "Did you tell me he's Romanian?"

"His parents are from Romania, yes."

"Then it makes sense."

"Can you make him forget?" Annie asked, beginning to realize the gravity of the situation.

"I don't think so. He's so scared he'll keep his distance. With all the people here, I can't risk making a scene. Can't grab him by the collar and force him outside, or into another room. It's best if we leave. Or, at least, if I leave."

"But we've only been here a short time."

"I'll go. Stay and do what you need to do here. I'm sorry, Annie. A creature like me doesn't belong in polite society." His eyes had turned stark, filled with shame and anger. "I'll wait for you. Take all the time you want."

He wound his way through the mingling guests and walked out the door. Annie stood still for a moment as people milled around her, recovering her wits from this unexpected turn of events. How had Florescu recognized so quickly that Rafael was a vampire? How would he know by just one look? Could Rafael have been mistaken in his interpretation of what he read in Florescu's mind for that brief instant?

But the blood had indeed seemed to drain from the professor's face and he did back away and rush off in a panic. Rafael hadn't seemed scary to anyone else at the party. What was with Florescu? She decided to ask him, see if she could get to the bottom of all this.

Annie walked across the room to a hallway she'd seen the lanky professor escape to. She peeked into what looked like a guest bedroom, where coats had been thrown on the bed by partygoers. And there she saw him, sitting on an elegantly upholstered chair in one corner, taking long breaths as if trying to recover from his deep fright. Some color had come back in his narrow face. When he saw her, he jumped out of the chair.

"I'm alone," she told him, stepping into the room. "Are you okay?"

"Are you crazy?" he countered. "How could you bring that vile being into our midst? Do you know what he is? Do you?"

"What do you mean?" she asked, keeping her cool.

"Has he got you mesmerized? I knew enough not to let him invade my mind. You stupid woman!"

"Now, wait a minute. Let's try to stay calm. Why do you have all these suspicions about Rafael? Everyone else here who met him loved him."

"They don't know what I do about vampires," Florescu argued. "They don't even believe in a paranormal world. That the undead exist. My grandfather in Romania knew for a fact that vampires walk among us. When I was a child he told me he'd seen one himself. He described how their teeth look. How they can't be seen in mirrors. A camera can't capture their likeness. As soon as that kid taking pictures said he couldn't see Rafael in his photos, I knew he must be one of the undead. Even the kid knew he wasn't normal."

"Didn't you know there's a new app?" Annie improvised. "It prevents a person from showing up in photos, if they don't want to be photographed."

"A new app?" Florescu didn't seem to know whether to believe her or not. "Doesn't matter. When you introduced me, the first thing I saw were his fangs. Nothing can hide those." He suddenly reached out and pushed aside the collar of her suit. "Has he bitten you? Are you under his power?"

"No." Annie pulled back her collar on both sides of her neck. "See? I'm untouched. Because you're mistaken about Rafael," she asserted, knowing she was lying.

"You're a fool!"

"No, you are," she shot back, angry now.

"I don't *think* so," he said with contempt. "And you want to be promoted to full professor. You, involved in an evil liaison. If you know what's good for you, you ought to take back your request for promotion. If you don't, word may get out that your mystery man is one of the undead. Information I'm sure neither you nor he would want exposed."

"Now you're threatening me? Just so you can get promoted instead of me?" Annie sensed by the anxiety in his hazel eyes that he was intimidated by her. His hostile bluster she perceived to be his method of getting the upper hand.

"There are a lot of associate professors who would like to be promoted," he said, asserting himself even more by edging a sneer into his tone. "Why would I threaten you? I'm saying it's for the good of the university that a woman with your sordid life not become a full professor."

"We both know there's only going to be one promotion this year, and it's between you and me," Annie told him. "And you don't think I deserve it because I'm a woman, never mind who my boyfriend is."

"*What* your boyfriend is," he corrected her. "You stand warned. If you don't withdraw, everyone will know you're in a sexual relationship with a vampire."

"And who will believe you?"

He straightened to his full, impressive height. "I'm a well-respected professor here, more senior than you, you little upstart. Of course anything I say will be taken seriously."

"But you just told me yourself that others don't believe in a paranormal world," she calmly argued.

"Then I will educate them. In Eastern Europe even today there are those who know vampires exist "

Annie took in a long breath, wondering what to make of his contentions. "Well, I think we're done here. I'm not withdrawing my request for promotion. You do whatever you want."

She turned then and walked confidently out of the room.

But then she left the house without saying goodbye to anyone.

#

Filled with anger and remorse, Rafael sat in the passenger seat of Annie's pickup. Florescu had recognized he was a vampire and had immediately drawn the conclusion that he was evil. Maybe unevolved vampires in Transylvania were malevolent. But there existed those who had made an effort to overcome their bloodlust and find ways to be almost human. In truth, Rafael had never met another vampire. He'd remained isolated in the American Southwest, where few existed. But he'd read all he could. He'd even come across a rumor that a well-known playwright in Chicago might be, or have been, a vampire.

But beliefs and prejudices remained, and there was little Rafael could do about it. He felt guilty bringing all this into Annie's life. She shouldn't have to deal with these issues. Her only crime was to have fallen in love with him.

He saw Annie come around the front of the truck. As she opened the door and got in behind the wheel, he couldn't help but see the concerned look on her face.

"What's wrong?" he asked, filled with anxiety for her.

"Oh, it's nothing," she said in a tone that didn't quite sound as nonchalant as she probably hoped.

"Tell me."

She sighed in a reluctant way. "I found Frank Florescu sitting alone in a room down the hall. I decided to confront him. He was still shaken from meeting you."

"What did he say?"

"That if I don't withdraw my bid to become a full professor, word would get out that my boyfriend is a vampire. Remember I told you he and I are up for the same promotion? Well, he's using his fright of you to scare me out of the competition."

Rafael's shoulders sank. He'd feared the worst and this was it.

"If I find out where he lives," Annie said, "could you go to him and make him forget?"

Rafael leaned his head against the high back of his seat. "I could try. But I think it would be useless. He knows if I make eye contact, I can get into his head. Even if I pin him against a wall, he'll avert his gaze or close his eyes. I could take his blood and put him under my power, but after Inez, I don't want to do that to people anymore. It's my hope to transcend my vampire ways, especially now that we're together."

Annie shook her head. "No, I wouldn't want you to do that. If only because he may tell someone tonight that you're a vampire. I challenged him to, figuring no one would believe him. But if he tells people, and then he shows up next week with two marks on his neck, well that would be proof, wouldn't it?"

"Yes, it would," Rafael agreed, his spirit sinking. "I'm so sorry, Annie. I hope I haven't ruined your chances. Getting that promotion means a lot to you."

"You mean more to me," she said, taking his hand. "Don't worry. We'll figure this out."

He smiled at her sweet reassurance. But he feared there might not be any solution that would remedy the harm he'd done, just by accompanying her to a gathering of mortals. What was he thinking, to let her talk him into it?

Chapter Ten

Rafael's remorse only grew deeper in the days that followed. Annie had continued in her optimism that Florescu's knowledge of Rafael's nature would not hinder her career. She continued to insist he'd have no credibility if he told his colleagues. But Rafael wondered if she should feel so secure. He'd spent his whole existence on guard of having his dreadful secret discovered. It was why, when anyone got too close to him, male or female, he would take the necessary steps to put them under his power, so he could be in their mind and control what they said and did. Living on Rancho de la Noche, which was rather remote, he felt he had the protection he needed from the outside world. But Annie, who was from that world, had entered his domain, and he had fallen hard for her. He wanted her near forever. But he also wanted everything that was best for her, that would contribute to her happiness. How was that to be? How could his presence in her life be compatible with a happy future for her?

No, it's impossible. His final conclusion pained him as he sat on his couch next to Annie one evening, while she talked on her cell phone to one of her colleagues. Someone named Joan had called, and from Annie's side of the conversation, he could tell they were talking about Florescu. Rafael could gather that apparently Florescu had begun to spread the word that the man in Annie's life was a vampire. He heard her laugh and say to Joan, "Isn't that ridiculous?"

Now Annie was lying for him. Rafael absorbed this with deep chagrin. A dangerous situation had clearly gotten worse. He had to do something. He loved Annie too much to ruin her life. There was only one solution.

Tears stung the backs of his eyes as Annie said goodbye and ended the call. He blinked them away, knowing he had to be strong and resolute.

"That was my friend, Joan. She was at the party. I don't think I had the chance to introduce you," Annie said, upbeat and smiling. "But she noticed you and thought you were handsome."

"Thanks," Rafael said. "You were talking to her about Florescu, weren't you?"

Annie's smile diminished. "Yes. Joan heard that Frank has been quietly telling people that my boyfriend is a vampire. He didn't say that to Joan directly. He knows she and I are close friends. But he did tell Tom Harvey, another professor who is her good friend and mine. And Tom told Joan that Florescu has put out his vampire theory to other colleagues, too, particularly those on the award committee. If he can cut me out of the competition, he'd win, and that would set him up for the promotion to full professor."

Rafael looked at her, aghast. "Aren't you concerned? You're so lighthearted about it."

"Because I don't think anyone will believe Florescu. Joan didn't. She was laughing about it. Said she thinks Frank is off his rocker. He's only doing himself harm, not me."

Rafael rubbed his hand over his eyes. He turned toward Annie and as he spoke his voice came out harrowed and grave. "You need to take this much more seriously. This could ruin your future. It's no use, Annie. We can't stay together. I need to be out of your way, or you'll never have a successful life."

"What do you mean?" Annie asked, her voice constricting with emotion. "We have to be together. I love you."

"And I love you," he said, taking her hand. "Too much to destroy you. Leave me. Go back to your place in Tucson."

Annie shook her head, her eyes filled with disbelief. "No one at the university needs to know where I live. That's irrelevant to who wins any award or gets a promotion."

"What I mean is, we have to part," Rafael explained with great sorrow. "My presence in your life will be your downfall. It's already starting. We must say goodbye, forever, while there's still a chance that you can regain all you've worked for."

"Goodbye forever," she repeated in a whisper. Tears glazed her eyes as she looked at him imploringly. "How can you say that?"

"With dread and sorrow, but that's how it must be. It seems I need to do the thinking for both of us. You are failing to grasp the tragic outcome you face if we stay together. I had a hurtful impact on Inez's life, and on others before her. I love you too much to do that to you. We must part and never see each other again."

Annie stared at him, speechless, tears spilling from her eyes.

"Maybe you should go back to Brent. If he truly loves you, he might still marry you. Then you can have the family life you once told me you wanted. You can be a stepmother for Zoe."

Annie blinked hard. "Marry Brent? But then I'd be living on the ranch next to you, and we're to never see each other again? How would we keep our distance, with a love as strong as ours?" She wiped away a tear with shaking fingers, but her eyes grew steely. She pulled her other hand out of his. "Unless what you're really saying is you don't want me anymore. Be honest. Have you grown tired of me?"

Rafael adamantly shook his head. "Of course not. I love you more than I've ever loved anyone. It's exactly *because* I love you so much, I need to exit your life. Before any more damage is done on my account. I'm . . . I'm considering leaving here. Moving to Spain where I was born," he improvised. "So there is no chance you will encounter me, at the ruin or anywhere."

She drew her head back, doubt in her eyes. "How would you travel to Spain?"

"Have myself shipped. I'll find a way."

"But you have no place to rest there. And what about Rancho de la Noche?"

"My foreman and Francisco will keep the ranch going for me. It's a small world nowadays. I can be in another country and still keep the ranch." Rafael didn't have a ready answer to her point that he'd have no place to rest in Spain. He, of course, had no intention of moving. He'd stay and secretly keep an eye on Annie, but he needed her to think he'd left the territory so she wouldn't try to see him.

"How can you do this to me?" she asked, her voice shattering as new tears spilled down her cheeks, breaking his heart. "How can you say I should marry Brent?"

"If not him, find someone else to marry. I want you to have what you used to say you wanted, a family of your own. You're still young. If you stay with me, you'll age, your chances of having children will fade, and your career may be demolished. I won't do that to you. Leaving me is for your own good. Don't you see?"

"No! All I see is that you don't love me, or you wouldn't push me away like this. You've said you've had many women over the centuries. Is that because you get bored and look for someone new? Is that what's happened? I hadn't realized you could be so fickle. Were you put off by the party I made you go to, when everything went wrong? I'm too much trouble, is that it?"

She got up and stood in front of him, her voice full of accusation. "Your love has faded and you're making all this up to let me down easy. You no longer feel the way you did the night you begged me not to marry Brent. Now you have the nerve to suggest I should go back to him. I never, ever, dreamed you could be this heartless and cold."

Her words wounded Rafael to the core. He still wanted, needed her love, and it grieved him to think that she was forming this awful opinion of him. But perhaps it was for the best that she think less of him. It would prevent her from trying to renew their relationship. He couldn't let his eternal loneliness, his desperate desire for her, get in the way of protecting her from himself. If he couldn't do that, he wasn't truly loving her in the selfless way he should.

Rafael lowered his eyes, unable to look at her just then. "I *am* heartless and cold. It's the nature of a vampire. I may become enamored, even love someone, but my true self always reappears. I survive on blood, Annie. I use and manipulate people for my own purposes. I fell for you, but it needs to be over now between us. I promise you, you're better off without me."

Annie remained silent for a long moment. He kept his eyes averted, but eventually he heard her harsh whisper.

"You are callous and cruel to hurt me this way," she told him. "If you don't love me, why not just say so, instead of making up all this stuff about how it's for my own good? If you really had my welfare at heart, you'd never sever our relationship. Because I can't be happy without you. Knowing the love we've shared, how could I ever be content with some other man? Even now with the cold things you've said, I still want only you."

Frustrated that she was still arguing, Rafael rose from the couch and stepped away from her, shaking his head. He wished she would leave and not prolong this. His inner resolve, his willpower, was beginning to crumble. He needed this to be over and done. Or he might take it all back, ask her forgiveness and beg her to stay.

"Oh, don't worry," she said, angry now as she headed toward the bedroom. "I'll pack my stuff. I won't stay where I'm clearly not wanted. I'll be out of your way in twenty minutes."

In less than fifteen minutes, she'd haphazardly gathered her things and walked out of his house. Rafael pushed aside the curtains on the window by his front door and watched her truck drive away. When the lights of her pickup had disappeared from view, he sank to the cold, tile floor, bereft and alone once again. But the aching pain in his heart was balanced by the fact that he'd done the right thing for the woman he loved beyond all measure.

Chapter Eleven

Christmas came and went. Annie spent the holiday with an elderly aunt who lived south of Tucson. Aunt Gracie was all the family Annie had left. With Rafael out of her life, Annie wondered what she should do. What would her future be? Should she focus on finding a husband? Not Brent, as Rafael had suggested. She was over Brent, now that she'd glimpsed his nasty side. And how could she be as devoted to any other man as she'd been to Rafael? Marriage seemed a dim option. Maybe she should adopt a child and be a single parent.

Annie wouldn't have been entertaining any of these ideas if she were still with Rafael. He'd filled her life. But now her days seemed empty, and depression threatened to overcome her. She needed to combat her forebodings of a lonely future with some sort of positive action. Fortunately classes would start again soon. Teaching would help fill the void.

Her excavation of the ruin had come to a halt. Temporarily, she hoped. Not because Brent was threatening to prevent her. She simply couldn't bear to go to the Anasazi site because it brought back too many memories. She needed to get over Rafael. Somehow. Perhaps she needed to adopt Inez's philosophy, that habit replaces happiness.

On the first morning that classes resumed at the university in mid-January, Annie went to her office, dressed in a calf-length, black wool skirt and a gray sweater set. In the hallway, she ran into Joan, similarly dressed, only her sweater set was blue.

"Hey, we're almost twins," Joan said.

Annie made the effort to smile, and tried to sound upbeat. "Great minds think alike," she quipped.

"What's wrong?" Joan immediately asked. "You seem a little down."

Joan had always been an intuitive person. Annie hesitated, wondering how much to say.

"Anything I can do to help?" Joan asked with empathy.

Annie shook her head. "Rafael and I aren't together anymore."

"Oh, I'm sorry to hear that," Joan lamented. "Here, let me give you a hug."

The two women embraced.

Annie blinked back tears. "It's been almost a month. I ought to be getting over it by now."

"That's not much time," Joan said. "You're here, you look great, you're moving on. Be proud of yourself."

Annie appreciated her friend's support and reassurance, but underneath she still felt bereaved, knowing her life would never be the same.

At that moment, Tom came down the hall. When he saw Annie and Joan, he was all smiles. "Hey, did you hear the news?"

"What news?" Joan said.

"I just came from the department offices. Saw the announcement letter the secretary is mailing out right now. Annie, you've won the Outstanding Contribution to the Field of Archeology Award. Congratulations!"

Tom reached out and shook her hand. Joan gave her another hug.

Annie's mind was spinning. She'd pretty much forgotten about the award, her mind being so preoccupied trying to understand why Rafael sent her away.

"Really? I won?"

"You won," Tom repeated, laughing. "You deserve it."

"Frank Florescu won't be happy," Annie said.

Tom shrugged. "No, but he's only got himself to blame. He ruined any chance he may have had by spreading unbelievable rumors."

Annie's hands grew cold. "I know. Joan told me."

"Rafael is out of her life now," Joan said to Tom. "It's too bad Frank made all those ridiculous accusations. He's become little more than a crackpot."

"True," Tom said, nodding. He sighed and looked at Annie. "So you've heard that Florescu was spreading the rumor that your guy was a vampire." Tom snickered. "Everyone's been laughing behind Frank's back. I even told him he should make an appointment with a psychiatrist. I think he'll be viewed as way too eccentric to be promoted to full professor."

"And now that you've won the award," Joan said to Annie, "you're a shoo-in."

Annie remained quiet for a moment, thinking, *It's just as I predicted. No one believed the arrogant Dr. Florescu.*

Why hadn't Rafael trusted her judgement?

"I hope so," Annie said, her emotions rising from relief to renewed optimism. But she still felt anger toward Rafael for his lame reason to end their relationship. "When will they announce the promotion? The first faculty meeting?"

"That's what I hear," Tom said. "Next week."

# # #

A week later, after finishing teaching her classes by mid-afternoon, Annie got in her truck and headed north toward Rancho de la Noche. Being mid-winter, the sun was setting early. She'd be able to confront Rafael and drive home again before midnight.

At the faculty meeting the day before, Dr. Hogan had announced the news. He'd smiled upon Annie as he invited everyone to applaud their new full professor, Dr. Annie Carmichael. Annie had blushed a bit as everyone did applaud, except for Frank Florescu, who could not seem to bring his hands together to join in. He'd looked totally flummoxed, like the rug had been pulled out from under him. Apparently he'd been positive his gossip strategy would work.

Feeling good about herself and her academic future, Annie had decided late last night to tell Rafael that his fears for her had not come about. She wondered what his reaction would be.

The sun had set by the time she drove up to Rafael's ranch house. Lights were on inside. Apparently he hadn't gone to Spain. What new tactic might he come up with now? All she wanted was the truth.

# # #

Rafael was contemplating how to pass another lonely night after briefly meeting with his foreman and Francisco shortly after sundown. What should he do? How did he while away time before he'd met Annie? He'd ride Esperanza across the chaparral in the moonlight. Or shape-shift and run as a wolf. Go into town and rob the blood bank. Which reminded him that he needed to make a monetary donation to the blood bank, his way of making amends for stealing from them several times a year.

As he pondered his choices, he sighed and decided to stay in and finish reading *Persuasion*. Annie had said that Jane Austen was her favorite author. He'd ordered several Austen books online.

Ordinarily such delicate, female-oriented novels would not be to his taste. But he'd found that reading them made him feel closer to Annie. Though he'd parted from her for good, he still longed for her. And the books also seemed to bring out a remnant of his lost humanity, which he needed to combat his vampire nature.

He sat on the couch and began reading Chapter 20 of his book. He paused to reread a line of dialogue Captain Wentworth said:

A man does not recover from such a devotion of the heart to such a woman! He ought not; he does not.

The words captured Rafael's current state of mind perfectly. Imagine that. Jane Austen would have understood him.

Suddenly he heard the crackling sound of a vehicle on his gravel driveway. In a few moments a knock came at the door. Wondering who it could be, Rafael reluctantly set the book aside and got up to answer it. Perhaps it was his foreman on his way home, stopping because he'd forgotten some ranch business he meant to discuss at their meeting earlier.

Raphael opened the door. He saw before him the one beloved face he'd told himself he wished he could forget, but instead had worked to remember and cherish.

"Annie." His voice came out a perplexed whisper. "Why . . . ? You're not supposed to be here."

"Well, I *am* here," she countered. "I just want a short conversation, to straighten out a few things."

There was such a tough resilience in her eyes that he could not find the wherewithal to argue. In truth, he wanted to take her in his arms and bless her for the opportunity just to look at her again.

He opened the door wider and stepped aside to let her in.

She turned to him as he shut the door. "So you haven't gone to Spain."

"No . . . not yet." He had no plans to leave, but he wasn't about to admit that. "What do you want to straighten out with me?"

"You need to know that you were all wrong about Frank Florescu telling everyone you're a vampire."

"He didn't say anything?"

"Oh, yes, he did. But no one believed him. My colleagues think he's gone nutty. So I won the award. I've also been promoted to full professor."

Rafael felt so relieved and joyful for her that he wanted to embrace her. Nevertheless, he didn't. He needed to stick to his principles. This episode may have turned out in her favor, but future events might still hinder her if he came back into her life.

"Wonderful, Annie. I'm happy for you."

"So," she continued, "the reason you gave for pushing me away didn't happen. What I want to know is, was that your real reason? You wanted to do the honorable thing and break up with me to save my career? That excuse is gone now. Did you send me packing because you had fallen out of love with me? If so, then tell me. If you don't love me, I'll give up on you. But if you do love me, then there is no reason for us to be apart. I love you and I'll never get over you." Tears welled in Annie's eyes. "So that's all I want, the unvarnished truth."

Rafael's heart swelled within his chest. His conviction that she would be better off without him faded. He loved her strength, the way she stood up to him and challenged him. It was what he admired about her from the very moment he met her at the ruin.

Wetness glazed his own eyes. "I never stopped loving you. That's the truth. I've missed you terribly. I'm totally and wretchedly miserable without you."

Her face crumpled into tears. He pulled her to him and she wept on his shoulder.

"I only meant to protect you," he said, stroking her slender back.

She pulled away to look at him. "You're sure? We can be together again?"

He smiled. "Yes, I need you here, living with me." He shook his head, marveling at the coincidence. "Before you knocked, I'd just read something Jane Austen wrote: 'A man does not recover from such a devotion of the heart to such a woman.'"

"That's bcautiful."

"That's my truth in a nutshell," he told her. "Believe it for the rest of your life."

Annie blinked back more tears, but smiled through them. "You're reading Jane Austen?"

"Because you like her." He glanced away as a new conviction entered his mind. His eyes met hers again. "All that's happened has made me wish more than ever to be mortal again. Not an oddity, outside the natural order. I want to be a part of society, an ordinary man. If we're to be together, then I need to escape my vampire curse."

Annie's expression changed. "Not on my account. I love you as you are."

"I know. But I don't love me as I am. I want us to live together as equals, not mortal and immortal. It just doesn't work. If I become mortal, we could marry. If I'm fully human again, we might even have a child together."

Annie's face had grown troubled. "But how? The Indian shaman you told me about?"

Rafael nodded. "He had a ritual he could perform that he believed would cure me. Inez feared I might perish. I hesitated and didn't go through with it. But I want to now."

"B-but what if you do perish?"

He touched her nose with his. "I'll come back and haunt you."

"It's not funny," she said. "I don't want to risk losing you."

He took her by the shoulders. "Annie, I've changed. You've changed me. This is something I need to do. For us. It's the only way. Please try to understand."

Annie bowed her head, new tears streaming down her cheeks. "All right," she whispered, "if that's what you want." She looked up. "I want you to be happy." She swallowed. "You know, I'm willing to let you turn me. We could be together forever then."

He shook his head. "No, I would never make you what I am. Gaining superhuman power is exhilarating. But it's a dark and vicious way to exist. Living on blood, separated from God. No, I would not subject you to that. Never."

Chapter Twelve

A few nights later, Rafael, Annie, and Inez drove together to the shaman's home at the edge of the nearby reservation. Rafael had convinced Inez to direct them to Joe Strongwalker's house, as she had taken Rafael to meet him many years ago. Inez had reluctantly agreed. He felt buoyant with new hope that the shaman could cure him of his curse and make him mortal again.

As they stood in front of the door at the modest adobe home, Rafael glanced at Annie. She looked grave and apprehensive. Inez wore a similar expression. He wished they wouldn't worry. Everything would turn out fine. He just knew it would. Annie had come back to him. His worries on her account had not come about. Everything was going well for a change, and he felt confident and optimistic.

Rafael knocked on the door. In a few moments, a plump, elderly woman, dressed in a long skirt and denim jacket, answered.

Inez spoke up. "Hello, Rosa. Perhaps you remember me. I'm Inez Garcia. We've come to see your husband. We met with him years ago. He believed he could cure my friend, Rafael."

"I remember." Rosa sadly shook her head. "He's gone. My husband, Joe, died five months ago."

Inez took a step backward. "Oh, I'm so sorry."

Rafael absorbed this information with shock. He felt disoriented for an instant, so trusting he'd been in the belief that soon he would be changed into a mortal. He nodded to the lady as Inez and Annie bid her goodbye. They turned and slowly walked back to the pickup. No one said anything for a few long minutes.

When they reached the truck, Annie stopped and took hold of his arm. "I'm sorry you didn't get your wish. But I'm happy with the way things are."

Rafael turned to look at Annie, then at Inez. "Both of you are relieved, I can tell." Their reaction miffed him a bit. He felt exactly the opposite of relieved.

Neither woman replied to his comment, their silence confirming the truth of his observation.

"Your story isn't over yet," Inez quietly told him. "We Indians have long legends and stories that take forever to tell. It's the same for you, Rafael. You and Annie have each other. Let your story continue. The future will take care of itself."

"I agree with Inez," Annie said. "Maybe someday we'll find out about another cure. Maybe there's another shaman who knows the secret ritual. If I need to become like you so we can continue as soul mates, then that will become clear as time goes on."

"For me, time has already been going on forever," Rafael said, head bowed.

Another setback. He'd had so many in his time on the planet. He supposed he could overcome this one, too.

At least he no longer felt so alone. Rafael lifted his chin and gazed up at the stars in the night sky twinkling down on them. Even darkness had some beauty.

He pulled Annie close and took hold of Inez's hand. "If He could hear me, I'd thank God for both of you," he assured them. "We'll go on. See what the future brings."

About the Author

Lori Herter grew up in the suburbs of Chicago, graduated from the University of Illinois, Chicago Campus, and worked for several years at the Chicago Association of Commerce & Industry. She married her husband, Jerry, a CPA, and they moved to Southern California a few decades ago. They still live there with their cat, Jasmine. They have traveled extensively in the U.S., Canada, Europe, New Zealand, Australia, and Tahiti. Lori's favorite destination of all is Ireland.

Lori has written romance novels published by Dell Candlelight Romances, Silhouette, and Harlequin. Some of these books are currently available as ebooks on Amazon and Barnes & Noble. She also wrote a four-book romantic vampire series published by Berkley with the titles OBSESSION, POSSESSION, CONFESSION, and ETERNITY. Her most recent work published by Berkley is her novella, "Cimarron Spirit" in the vampire anthology, EDGE OF DARKNESS. "Cimarron Secrets" is the sequel to "Cimarron Spirit." Watch for the third novella in the Cimarron Series, "Cimarron Seductress."

Lori's website is: www.loriherter.com

Watch for the next novella in Lori Herter's
Cimarron Series:

CIMARRON SEDUCTRESS

An old flame returns to
vampire Rafael de la Vega

11924039R00082

Printed in Great Britain
by Amazon.co.uk, Ltd.,
Marston Gate.